SAT® VOCABULARY BUILDING
NOVEL TRILOGY

D1235314

FEAR NONE

BUT

THE INNOCENT

by   Raymond Karelitz &
     T. J. Falcone

© 1988, 1994, 2003 (revised/edited)
2005 (enhanced vocabulary)
by Raymond Karelitz /
Hi-Lite Publishing Company

SAT® *VOCABULARY BUILDING-NOVEL TRILOGY:*
Fear None But the Innocent

This book may be purchased in quantity for classroom use. Contact the publisher for discount rates.

Copyright © 2005 by Raymond Karelitz
Hi-Lite Publishing Company
P.O. Box 240161
Honolulu, Hawaii 96824

All characters in this book are fictional. Any similarity between characters and events with actual events is purely coincidental.

Library of Congress Catalogue Card Number: 2005926630

Karelitz, Raymond
Falcone, T. J.

SAT Vocabulary-Building Novel Trilogy: Fear None But The Innocent

Summary:
Jeremy recounts how the friendship between Danny and him survived through good and bad times, and what eventually forced them to travel in different paths.

[1. Teenage Exploits - Fiction   2. Friendship - Fiction]
I.   Title

ISBN 1-56391-021-7

Reading Level: Grades 10+

PRINTED IN THE U.S.A.

Second Printing
Revised Edition

A mysterious fire erupted at Saint Paul School during the night of the Junior prom, but only Jeremy knows the complete story.

Danny had made it clear no one would get the better of him.

Now, in the ruins of the buildings, Jeremy warns the world why we should *Fear None But The Innocent.*

FEAR NONE BUT THE INNOCENT

Special Textbook-Edition featuring

•enhanced text for vocabulary building

•attractive illustrations

•end-of-book *Glossary*

(160 pages)

Computer Layout:	Toni Shortsleeve
Illustrated by:	Dexter Doi
Cover Design:	Doug Behrens

TABLE OF CONTENTS

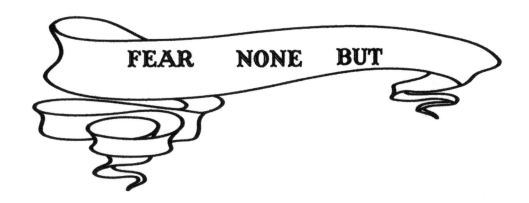

FEAR NONE BUT

Reading and building key vocabulary is a pleasurable experience when the stories are exciting and the text is challenging.

The enclosed tale is set in the Hawaiian Islands, but the adventures and lessons learned are universal.

Come let the Huckleberry Finn in you escape on a raft of unbounded fantasy and imagination as you embark on a verbally enriching odyssey with characters who will endear themselves to you through their personal and poignant escapades.

Let the journey begin...

THE INNOCENT

CHAPTER I
An Introduction

Nobody really knew what happened. The newspapers and the radio reports never revealed the truth. Everyone was more interested in hearing what they wanted rather than learning what really **transpired**. To the public, the entire event was but a regrettable tragedy for the school. Nobody ever suspected that the school was the **culprit** and that it destroyed a teenager's life in the process. Or if the press did know, they surely weren't about to tell the real story. The public wouldn't have wanted to hear it, anyway.

I guess it really all began when the Hawaiian summer was nearing and we were looking forward to the completion of our Sophomore year with all the dreams of **grandeur** that accompany any upper classman. When we received our class rings in May, we began the journey straight for adulthood, prom and all. But I never fully realized that Danny wasn't interested in becoming a compromising adult. Danny and I had unique ideals, and we both became victims of our own beliefs, each in a different way. Danny strove for identity, I clung to security; and on that hot, sticky Saturday evening, we each etched our future against the outline of the clouds.

I was there when the pressures came together to destroy Danny. I saw the hurt building up through the months as he sought direction in a world of systems and **conformities**. Nobody had to explain to me that he was being treated unjustly. After all, I was his best friend. I still am his best friend. I'll always be his best friend.

If only he had trusted me and **confided** in me, if only he hadn't thought he was so **utterly** alone. I suffered as he did, but he was the one who couldn't compromise, couldn't hold it in. When the science teacher finally pushed him over the edge, the game was over and the hopes and dreams we'd **chimerically contemplated** could no longer ever **materialize**.

Danny and the whole world came together, face to face, in the tenth grade. He lost the battle, but his words will live on forever at Saint Paul School. The school teachers and officials may never know what really happened, but the words are there for all to understand.

It's hard to recall what really started the bomb ticking, what seemed to break an otherwise **undaunted** spirit. Maybe it was Sarah – she was his only **confidante**. I was there, but I could only observe and wonder what was really going on beneath his **suave** and **nonchalant** exterior. I knew there was a fuse, and yet I couldn't alter the **inevitable**.

Danny was always a **zealous iconoclast**, never **heeding** teachers' advice but choosing instead to follow his own **distorted** guidance. In the ninth grade, he purposely placed his chewing gum on Mr. Samson's chair, and the **rickety** old man fell into the trap just as he was wrapping up his Pythagorean theorem discussion. We joked that, even though the whole class was 'stuck,' the teacher got it 'in the end'. It **enlivened** the class, but it didn't quench Danny's appetite for pranking around. We called it "pranking," just like car thieves might call their art "borrowing." I think we all knew it was more than just kicks. For me it was a phase, a time in my life during which I **immersed** myself but eventually graduated from such **puerile** and **asinine antics** and then began the process of **maturation.** But for Danny it was the start of something bigger and better. Funny how I even today think of it as "better" – gosh, you'd think I learned my lesson by now.

Danny never actually got caught in the ninth grade or in the tenth, but he was nonetheless shamed and humiliated and fought back **valiantly** against those who sought to make him **grovel** and **truckle** to authority. His sweet revenge came finally when everyone had no choice but to listen to him. His story did indeed echo far beyond the school newspaper. Perhaps it was always his desire to become front-page news; and I guess I **unwittingly** helped him **realize** the dream. I only wish the papers knew the whole truth. But then again, they probably wouldn't have printed it – the reporters got their story and the school covered up its mistakes.

CHAPTER II
Changing Grades

Every school has its fraternities, its school committees, its honor societies and its group of trouble-makers. Danny and I became part of the 'trouble-makers,' enlisting in the least admired, though most feared club: the Striped Panthers.

Joining the Panthers **necessitated** being a ninth grader, a **feat** I almost didn't accomplish. It took the **coordinated** efforts of Danny and me to help me pass the eighth grade. And it also took a lot of luck.

Actually, I was never a bad student in school; I usually got A's and B's. But a host of things occupied my mind during the eighth grade. Mostly it was Danny. He had run into trouble maintaining his own minimum grades, and I went out of my way to assist. Perhaps I went too far, because as the school-year came to a close I found myself in a **precarious** and **problematic** position. I had no time to correct the **deficiency**, so I tried instead to **burrow** my way out of the **dilemma** through **artful** persuasion, combined with a few **underhanded** tricks. Danny, of course, provided the tricks.

Getting one's grades changed is no easy task. It requires just the right combination: a smile for one teacher and a tear for another. And even that doesn't always work. On my own, I managed to convince three of the teachers to spare me a D – Mrs. Proust even gave me a C out of the kindness of her guilt-ridden heart, perhaps because I had the guts to tell her how much I enjoyed her class. I think she probably dropped a dozen other students' grades when she raised mine. But as Danny said, that wasn't my problem.

Changing two other grades required Danny's assistance, a bit more creativity and a higher degree of risk. One wasn't so hard. Mr. Santiago was always **mawkish** when it came to the end of the year and the time neared to bid his students farewell. If he wasn't stoned, he sure was down on something. His eyes looked like he'd swum under water for an hour viewing the sea life below. Red streaks turned his brown and whites into purple and reds. The students would kid him – "Hey, Mr. Santiago, did you really paint your house last night...purple?" or "Gee, I'm sorry that you forgot to take off your purple shirt when you washed it." Nobody meant any harm by it all, but he was indeed a 'sight for sore eyes,' my contribution to the **inane** remarks.

Mr. Santiago's **vulnerability** played perfectly into our hands since he couldn't see very well behind those purple and whites. He still managed, however, to carry on his final day's classroom affairs as if it were just another day, complete with a lecture, textbook exercises and final entries into his grade book. Our interest, of course, lay solely in the grade book. And without too much effort, Danny managed to **divert** the entire class's attention while I **secured** the spiralbound book and changed a few critical homework grades. Danny had no problem drawing attention. It was as easy as 'pie,' which he so carefully had smuggled into class from the cafeteria and had so carelessly dropped five minutes before the class ended. Nobody would have guessed how many hours we had planned the event, but that was the challenge in those days: to get away with our pranks and never tell anyone our secret. We were special friends. We had enough **incriminating** stories about one another to get ourselves committed to an institution for life, but we knew we were not adults and that our **escapades** were merely childish games.

Mr. Santiago never suspected what we had done, but Mrs. Kilbraith wasn't quite so **gullible**, or blind. Yet, Danny and I pulled off the ultimate prank, changing my F to a B without her ever knowing. It wasn't easy, but with my brains and Danny's **clamoring** desire to be center-stage, it worked like a charm.

I can so clearly remember when Danny first 'accidentally' bumped into Linda Kilbraith. It was as if fate had **predestined** such perfect timing. But Danny and I knew better – we'd been rehearsing it for days.

"I'm not sure," I overheard her remark to Danny. "I don't even know you very well."

"But Linda, haven't I been your friend? When you needed extra paper, didn't I swipe George's and give it to you?"

"Yeah, but what does that have to do with movies? My mom doesn't want me to go out on school nights. And you know, you're not her favorite pupil either."

Lunchtime wasn't the most **opportune** moment to ask Linda out to a movie, but Danny and I knew that it was the only time available to **solicit** the request.

"Gee Linda, I like you. I've really never liked a girl as much as you. And you have such gorgeous light brown eyes."

"They're hazel, Danny, just like yours, and I don't know what you're getting at." Linda seemed **resolute** but then added, smiling, "Still, I like the way you carry on."

From then on, everything went as planned. Danny had **befriended** – or more accurately, **bamboozled** – Linda, had **engulfed** her with his magical charm and was now her date for the show. We knew Linda's mom wouldn't be home until 6:00, so Danny arranged the pick-up time for 5:00. It gave him an hour to be alone with her, survey the house and become familiar with its surroundings.

☆ ☆

"Gee Linda, your mom never really hated me," Danny said somewhat apologetically as he sat at her kitchen counter, eyeing her carefully. "I mean, I'm getting a C in English."

"From Mr. Chandler."

"Gee Linda, your mom never really hated me," Danny said somewhat apologetically.

"Yeah." Danny tugged at his blue jeans, waiting for the next **inexorably condemnatory** words from this girl he never even noticed before last week, the only person who ever told him what color his eyes really were. I don't think he ever knew he had hazel eyes.

"My mom kicked you out of her class for so many reasons that I seriously don't think she'll be happy to see you back in her life, especially not in her house."

The truth hurt a bit, but Danny knew his only **recourse** was to dismiss Linda's **blatant veracity** and concentrate on the task at hand. He could **ruminate** over the truth tomorrow; today he had better things to do. He was helping a friend, and when it came to friends nothing could **deter** his assistance.

"Well, I'm sorry for living," Danny added, casting a **pathetically** helpless-looking glance toward Linda, attempting to **elicit** some sympathy from her. "Does that make you feel better? I only wanted to try to be nice. You're a pretty stupid girl...to be hanging around me, anyway." Danny had little **tact** when he was **confronted**, but at least he got around it this time; Linda didn't catch on.

"Danny, I'm sorry. I guess you're not such a bad boy after all. It's just that my mom doesn't like students in the house. Especially not when it's near grade-time." She **peered** into his hazel whites, looking for a clue that might give away some real reason for his being in her house. Danny, of course, was way ahead of her.

"What, am I in your mom's class? Am I flunking her English class? Did I come here to try to rip off her grade book so I can change the grades?" The truth came so close, yet appeared so far away. This was one of the most challenging elements of pranking, to expose the truth in such a way that nobody would ever suspect. It was like approaching a fire but not getting burned. The idea of playing with the truth fascinated Danny, who **invariably** emerged victorious.

"I'm sorry Danny. I don't know why I said that. I guess I've been watching too many *Three's Company* reruns. You're really a sensitive boy, do you know that?"

☆ ☆

"Danny, where are you hiding? You should have been home an hour ago. I know you're somewhere in the house. I heard you come in."

Danny had to be a sensitive boy. He needed to know where his mom was, where his dad was, and what mood they each were in. 'Sensitive,' that was an understatement. He needed to be **psychic** to relate to all the changes and **hostilities** around him. His mom worked twelve hours a day selling life insurance, his dad meanwhile spent twelve hours a day drinking *Budweiser* while watching videos of every football game ever aired. His mom was the **indefatigable** breadwinner, his father the **perennially shiftless** and **slothful** couch potato. The relationship didn't make sense; it hadn't made sense since the day they were married, the month after Danny was born.

Danny had to be a sensitive boy

"Yeah mom, I'm here. I told you I'd be late. I had detention at school, that stupid Mr. Fartheim."

"Don't go speaking that way about your teachers, Danny. I've told you that school is good. You need to study study study. Don't follow your good-for-nothing excuse for a father. He's garbage, pure garbage. And if you want to be like him, then I don't want to see you again. Ever." And she meant it. Every word.

"I was just at Linda Kilbraith's house. You know, her mother teaches at Saint Paul." The truth got away from him, and he knew it wouldn't go unnoticed.

"You lying brat. Yesterday you tell me you are at detention, now you say you're at some made-up friend's house. You always lie, you and your good-for-nothing father. Lies, good-for-nothing lies. You better wash out your mouth, you'll become nothing but a good-for-nothing liar." She would always repeat herself for emphasis, but every word spoken clearly left its **indelible** mark on Danny. For all the help he offered me, he seemed to suffer repeatedly for it at home.

☆ ☆

Danny saw Linda during lunchtime every day that week, getting closer to her with each new "Hello." He kept me posted as he inched his way closer to her heart – and to the grade book. He seemed driven to finish what he had set out to do, reflecting an intense **meticulous** nature which **belied** his outward casual **countenance**. Nobody else seemed to sense the **compulsion** with which he sought victory, even as small a victory as changing a friend's grades. Sooner or later he would break out on his own. I knew it long before it happened, but I always lacked the courage to risk my security and join him in his **odyssey**. He wanted to accomplish more than I could ever even dream about. Danny was clearly my idol.

On Wednesday, Linda finally asked Danny over for dinner. "Heck, I'm no good for you. Your mom's probably told you a million things I've done wrong." The truth was always a challenge while pranking.

Linda didn't have a chance. She'd fallen for every word and reacted almost instinctively in a **maternalistic mien** of protective **succor** upon hearing such **self-deprecation**.

"Danny, you're so sweet. My mom doesn't know what she's saying most of the time. And anyway, why would I listen to her – she's only my mother. I believe you; I hope you understand what I mean." Tiny droplets formed as she attached herself dreamily to a new allegiance. Danny shrugged it off, focusing his attention instead toward his well-planned goal. He wasn't accustomed to seeing tears; crying and showing feelings of emotion didn't serve any purpose. Her expression only reminded him of days when even tears weren't enough to get his way.

✩ ✩

"Danny, why are you home late? Did you get into trouble again?" his mom **interrogated** in her **autocratic stentorian** voice. "Always problems at home and at school, and now what did you do? Steal something? Break something?"

There was no pause for Danny to reply, but he was accustomed to that. His mom didn't want any answers.

"You know, the police always come by here asking about you. What did you do now, huh boy? You bring me shame, nothing but shame. You and your good-for-nothing father. Let them take *him* away. Then I can live in peace. Both of you, bad people. Bad people." Kind words didn't come from his mom. She'd been raised in a poor village in Japan, had come to America with nothing in her pocket, married a Marine with the hope that she could escape to an easier life, but then found herself **toiling** endlessly to make ends meet. Fourteen years later, she had saved enough to buy a house, rear a child and support the entire family. But the experience left its bitterness, and Danny was the reminder of all her **labors**. To her, the results weren't worth the effort, and Danny felt the **denigrating** daggers whenever she'd open her mouth to **vent** her ever-present **wrath**.

"Yeah mom, I know," he'd answer **sheepishly** in the brief moment of silence. He had learned not to argue with her. She was the **de facto** head of the household, and as long as he wanted to live in her house, she was always right.

"And I told you to eat everything on that plate. No eat, no play." His mom didn't compromise. Never.

"But mom, I went to *7/Eleven* before I came home. I didn't know you were going to be home." Maybe the truth would help.

"Lies, always lies. I can't believe anything you say, so just shut up and eat."

No compromise, no understanding. Never.

✩ ✩

Dinner at the Kilbraith house was not what Danny had expected. There was praise, **conviviality** and sincere **compassion** in the **familial** conversation. Maybe Mrs. Kilbraith was right, he'd thought; maybe he was just a rotten kid who didn't know when it was time to grow up. The candied yams and the hot roast beef weren't merely TV-dinner microwave **concoctions**. They represented a day's worth of cooking, preparing and **savoring**. He'd heard others talk about family dinners, but for Danny the closest thing to a freshly cooked meal was *McDonald's*.

"But did you get my grades changed?" I asked him on Thursday.

9

"Look, I said the meal was good, but I didn't say I was stupid, did I?"

Sure enough, Danny and his hazel whites had found their way to the grade book on his way to the bathroom, having **perceptively espied** where the mother had laid it upon her return home after school. He'd already gotten the information **subtly** from the unsuspecting daughter on Wednesday, and when the mother came home he merely confirmed that it was rested in its proper place. From then on it was child's play, as easy as going to the bathroom, and Danny was once again heroic in his mission.

"Hey, and don't go telling anyone about my eyes, okay Jeremy? Or maybe I'll tell a few things about your brains." He didn't need to say any more. He wasn't kidding, and I knew when it was time to stop joking with him. He'd changed my grades, and whether or not Mrs. Kilbraith actually ever really noticed what we'd done, I got a B for her stupid English class and my problems were over.

CHAPTER III
Entering The Lair

Having barely survived the eighth grade with Danny's help, we both looked to our first official year of high school with high hopes. And the Striped Panthers seemed to represent the stepping stone offering us the **prominent** reputation we so eagerly sought.

The Striped Panthers of Saint Paul High met once a month after school, as had been the tradition for as many years as I can remember. We got **initiated** in the ninth grade, in the same manner as everyone else before us, pledging our loyalty to the club and promising to help one another against the '**oppression** of the outside world.' It really seemed as though we were now someone special, and we in turn **devoutly** though **naïvely** embraced ideals we hardly understood, ideals we dared not question. This new **solidarity** filled us with an **ineffable invincibility**, a feeling of self-worth we hadn't found at home or in class; for us the Striped Panthers **epitomized** the **quintessence** of friendship and togetherness.

Clint Hanson was the upperclassman who **whetted** our **recalcitrant** appetites and led us to cross the **proverbial** point of no return. He approached us during the first week of school, three months after I was spared the shame of repeating the year thanks to Danny's heroic rescue mission.

"Well, boys, are you interested?" he asked with **glacial indifference**, staring us both in the eyes, alternately, as I **assayed** this new and **hitherto** unexplored opportunity.

His icy inquiry left me somewhat **incredulous**. "Are the Striped Panthers really bad or are they perhaps a sort of Robin Hood group?" I wondered. "Do they cause trouble or are they really Boy Scouts in panther clothing?"

"I think it's a good idea. How about you, Mr. J.?" Danny advanced as I considered the options. Perhaps I detected some sort of **daredevil** attitude or maybe it was the way that Danny **intonated** his question, but I **tacitly** perceived that I was being told what to say. Having **contrived** and participated with him in **myriad** pranks, I knew when his words were meant in **jest**. Not this time. He was serious.

"Sure Danny, sounds pretty good to me," I **conceded** at last, "but what do we do?"

"Just come down to Miller's Annex after school on Friday," the **veteran** Panther continued. "Bring some old clothes. We've got some work for you boys to do." He **chortled demonically**, letting us catch just enough of his **sardonic sneer** to make me regret having committed myself quite so **readily**.

After Clint Hanson departed, I informed Danny of my **trepidation**. Danny wasn't affected, however. "Jeremy, you're not only a coward, you're a fool," he replied. "We've got those upperclassmen in our hands, and you're afraid of what they'll do to us. Man, you think the whole world's filled with people like us, but no way Jose. 'Cause we're the baddest, and ain't nobody gonna tell us what to do. You watch. You watch really good, Mr. J., 'cause this is Danny talking, and when I talk, people listen."

I knew he was right, but I never knew just how **ominously prophetic** the words would later become.

On Friday, I took along an extra change of clothes. I was prepared for the worst, figuring that I'd probably never wear any of them again. I hadn't slept as poorly since the time I was bitten by an eel during the summer and felt the **fury** of its fangs in my side several days thereafter. Dreams tend to **enhance** the best and worst thoughts in one's imagination, but for some strange reason we usually seem to **vividly** remember our dreams only when they are bad. I surely had my share the evening before **initiation**.

Danny came to school wearing his best on-the-town "threads," complete with velour pullover and **spiffy** white loafers. He looked like a tourist who just dropped by. The black pants with the striped shirt and white shoes were no doubt his **testimonial** for the school to know that he was indeed "bad." He would never let anyone limit his freedom to do what he wanted or wear whatever he preferred, and so I really wasn't surprised by what he wore to our **inaugural indoctrination**.

The Striped Panthers numbered twenty strong. They kept the membership **elite** by towing the line on the number of members, but because members were lost annually to graduation, recruiting was a necessary function for each new year.

Selecting Danny and me from the two hundred ninth-graders seemed very odd, leading me to suspect that not all incoming freshmen were anxious to join. Nevertheless, we were specially chosen, an honor in its own right. Unbeknownst to me at the time, Danny had already **executed** an assortment of **covert** activities under the **scrutiny** of the club's watchful eyes, faithfully **adhering** to its **perverse** and **misguidedly malignant modus operandi** long before Clint Hanson ever approached us. Danny had in the **interim** also made friends with Gerry Sanders, Bob Jacobson and Matt Small, the **latter** two representing, **collectively**, 450 pounds that nobody would dare seek to offend. The two were part of the Saint Paul Raider football team's **formidable** front line, and for club purposes they kept outsiders from becoming too close to the group's internal activities. **Ensuring** the bond of **solidarity** amongst the members themselves also required occasional bonecrushing; there was no voluntary withdrawal from the league.

At 2:40, Period 6 let out and I instinctively headed for Miller's Annex. The adjacent rooms housed the audio-visual materials, and I knew it to be unlike any other room in the islands – except perhaps a walk-in freezer. As the door opened, I could feel a rush of **frigid** air attacking my fingers. The setting, **obscured** by **subdued** lighting, provided the ideal atmosphere for a chilling experience.

Danny came to school wearing his best on-the-town "threads"...

Danny walked in right behind me, whispering in my ear as he sat down beside me. "It's our turn to rule," he said confidently, "so just sit back and enjoy the party."

The Panthers awaited, sixteen of the twenty returnees from the previous year. There had been much said about the **subterfuge** and **chicanery instigated** and **perpetrated** by the Panthers, and Father Conquistador had all-too-often threatened throughout the year to expel the president if the club did any more damage to any of the facilities. Without proof, however, the principal was powerless, and no students or teachers dared reveal the truth when the police were called in one Wednesday.

☆ ☆

I can remember that day of **reckoning** only too well, during the fourth quarter of the previous school year. We were at Alexander Theater, a newly constructed complex, pride of all the **alumni** who had been donating for years to have it built. And at long last we had our own theater, our own center for the performing arts. It had been officially opened a week prior, and the student body was **afforded** the opportunity to view the first full-length production, *A Midsummer Night's Dream*.

Josh Courtney was the club president that year, and the Panthers provided a memorable going-away present for their soon-departing Senior president the evening before. Their farewell festivity was innocent enough, but the Tuesday night **bacchanalian** bash left the members in a **semi-impervious** state of **bliss**, feelings of **infallibility predominant** amongst the striped animals. They were ripe for **rowdiness** on Wednesday.

The first scene of the play had barely survived the hisses and boos from the audience when Gerry Sanders, trouble-maker of the Junior class, turned from restless to **boisterous**. In the midst of some **inattentive** joking, Gerry was suddenly aroused by something said on stage. The cry for a character on stage had **piqued** his interest. **Puck** had been **summoned**, but **alas**, Gerry mistook it for a personal **affront**.

"What'd you call me?" he **bellowed** to whoever had unknowingly issued the **unwitting** verbal threat.

This was the cue for Mr. Farheim, Sociology teacher and part-time Assistant Dean of Discipline, to intercept and eliminate. Sanders was quickly escorted from the theater and subsequently suspended from school for a week, not so much for his disruption but for comments later **levied** against Farheim for his interference. Called everything from '**SS head-honcho**' to '**derelict** Jew,' Farheim had taken all he could from Sanders and his **brazen** band of merry men. Gerry became extinct for a week, but the Panthers moved on the prowl from the moment Farheim laid his hands on their fellow soldier.

14

No one dared tell the police who really slashed the seats and carved those **obscenities** on the back door of the theater, but everyone knew who was behind the daringly **egregious** acts of vandalism. The Panthers quickly gained **notoriety** for their brand of **vengefulness** which knew no limits. 'Don't get mad; get even' – one of Danny's pet phrases – became their club slogan, and even after Courtney's **reign** was through there was little doubt that the **toxic trend** would continue: Sanders was elected the next president.

☆ ☆

As I stood looking at sixteen of the most feared students at Saint Paul, I wondered specifically why they had chosen Danny and me, also curious whom the other two **inductees** would be. There was no reason for them to lower the number in the club – I know that animals gain strength in packs – but still I wondered why they wanted me to be part of it. After all, besides my lousy grades I didn't have an **M.O.** worthy of such **infamous** companionship. Perhaps Danny had made a special deal with them. I turned to get a sign from Danny, but he wasn't interested in what I was thinking. He had other ideas.

"Well, animals," Hanson began, "are you ready for some real action?"

My fingers began to warm up despite the **arctic** temperature of the annex. I felt my blood rushing through my head, reacting as if someone had placed a knife to my throat. I was scared.

Danny just stared **apathetically** at Hanson, looking up at his massive biceps which flexed in all the masculine authority he could **muster**. Danny wasn't impressed, and he showed it visibly.

"What's your problem, you **scrawny** little **whelp**?" Hanson **vociferated imperiously**. "You think I'm here to feed you porridge and soothe your stupid **infantile** ego?" He must have prepared a week to come up with that line.

"Look, Hanson," Danny said quietly and in an irritated tone, "you asked me and my pal to come, so get it over with. Otherwise we'll just walk out..."

"Walk out of here and you're dead meat." Hanson's true vocabulary was taking over. This was no time for **foolhardiness**, but I left Danny alone to do what he knew was best.

"Sanders, do you always let these clowns do your talking for you?" Danny stood up, but Hanson stepped in his tracks, looking down six inches right into Danny's hazel whites.

"Hanson, back off." Sanders words were *Gestapo*. Nobody thought to answer back, not Hanson, not anyone. Except perhaps Danny.

"Sanders, you got this goon to get me here, and if you want me in your sweet little party, I'm here. But if you don't, well, me and my own little friends here will just walk away."

Sixteen pairs of eyes stared at the bundle of cigarettes in Danny's cupped hands. My eyes were still glued on Hanson.

"Well, what do you say? Do we smoke, or do I blow?"

I never did discover what they had scripted for us, but then again, Danny knew it would never happen anyway. He'd planned the whole thing, and even Sanders couldn't control him. He had all the answers.

From that day forth Danny and I were Panthers, and we soon discovered that the once-a-month club gatherings were really **sub-rosa** strategy-meetings during which time **vindictive** schemes were hatched against anyone who had **maligned** a Panther. Teachers were the **principal** targets, but the list included parents, **meddlesome** students, even students from other schools. And one week, Danny added the police to the list of Panther victims.

CHAPTER IV
The Early Years

Danny and I didn't get into serious trouble simply because we were Panthers. True, the police were constantly **surveilling** us, but that wasn't for what we had done recently; it was for what we'd been doing for months. We had long since been a **prime** target of interest for the local blue-and-whites.

I never really had many problems when I was younger. Growing up in Hawaii was as **uneventful** for me as for all the other kids. I went to school regularly and then headed for the beach afterwards. Homework was a nightly chore that was routine and rather easy; the teachers became accustomed to **tailoring** homework around the beach, because anytime we were given excessive work to do, hardly a single boy would have the assignments completed. Surfing came first, and nobody else could reorganize our priorities. The experienced teachers simply adjusted and made the best of times; the unaccustomed either **adapted** or quit after a few years of frustration.

When I entered the fifth grade, I discovered another sport which soon **vied** for my attention: football. It became my obsession, either watching it or playing it. The strategies, the competitiveness and the physical activity **inundated** my senses and left me totally **fixated** upon the game. Surfing became my after-football recreation, and homework got pushed farther down the list of priorities. I wanted to be the best player on the team, in Hawaii, in the whole world. I had only one goal: to be the best. The word "best" took on new meaning. There was no "second best," only "best." The comparison for me was **analogous** to a mountain climber's distinction between successfully climbing the mountain or not climbing it to the top. One is victory and success; the other, failure without **consolation**.

I also discovered Danny in the fifth grade. He was a new student at Hawaiiana Elementary, having lived previously in Chicago for a few years. Before that, it really didn't matter. Nobody remembers much about their first few years simply because there's not much worth remembering. Life seems to "become" as one establishes oneself in the world. Before that it's just a **void**, a time to await entering the real world of identity and self-discovery.

I noticed Danny during one of our English quizzes, not an uncommon time to be looking around for new friends and some quiz-answers. Danny's eyes met mine, and we knew instantly that we had no answers to share. So instead, we began to share a friendship which **burgeoned** and **intensified** as the months progressed. We would chat during recess, **chide** and **chastise** teachers in **mock** fashion, and find ways to get the best grades with the least effort. These schemes turned eventually into a new form of strategy, the "prank." Originally, pranking was our way of tricking other people so that they would write incorrect answers on their quizzes and tests. Their mistakes helped lower the curve, and whatever was worse for others was better for us.

The fifth grade became a **pivotal** year for me – I found a new sport and a new friend. Danny's easy-going personality and eagerness to try something new and different made every day exciting and daring. We risked being caught in any of our numerous daily pranks, but our **sangfroid** and **savoir faire** got us off the hook whenever we were suspected of some wrongdoing.

Danny didn't touch football – he was not into that kind of sport. "You can go around and get your bones broken," he said to me one afternoon, "but I'll take care of Number One by sticking to surfing." I respected his survival-instinct, knowing all the while that I didn't want to compete against him, anyway. He was "Number One" in his world, while I struggled desperately and **perseveringly** to become "Number One" in my world of football.

It's hard to tell when our pranking became serious "trouble." We first began our pranks in the fifth grade, and after a couple years we perfected the art and increased the level of challenge. What began as a simple child's game turned into a real cops-and-robbers affair, of which we were the robbers. But we were only playing games, so it didn't really matter; we weren't committing **heinous** crimes. I guess we became more seriously involved as we became more **proficient** and the pranks more daring.

In the fifth grade, we had restricted our activities to after-school hours, clogging up the toilets with paper, sticking gum in the keyholes, **pilfering** pencils and changing report-card grades. But as the sixth grade began, our pranks took us to new lands beyond our neighborhood, granting us new **vistas** for our **waggish disportment** as we ventured into Waikiki on weekends. Penniless as we were then, we discovered a most **feasible** means for acquiring things we needed – such as skateboard wheels, candy and anything else that struck our fancy. To us it was known as the "five-finger discount" – nothing so boldly labeled as "stealing" – which we adopted as our newest form of pranking. That's when pranking began to mean more than fun and games; it meant survival and challenge.

The sixth grade passed smoothly and without any significant problems, a time in which I perfected my football and Danny perfected his pranking. But although we had different interests, we stuck close together in school and helped one another when it came to tests. We had code-words for every imaginable situation. In math, I displayed a most **ingenious** method of blinking, Danny nicknaming it "Math **Morse**." It was the kind of prank that fooled the teacher, fooled everyone else and made us closer friends than ever before. Every new trick, every idea that we kept to ourselves helped **bolster** and **reinforce** our relationship as true 'best friends.' We left Hawaiiana Elementary and entered Saint Paul School with an **indomitable** and **unwavering** allegiance, an **unimpugnable** bond of **mutual** trust and **unflagging** loyalty.

Nothing could change the feeling of security we felt. For Danny, our friendship marked a welcome change from his **prevailing** household of **animosity**, while I found Danny's individuality a challenge to my otherwise-pampered existence. Being an only child and **cherished** for that, I never had to worry about family conflicts or **problematic** situations involving me. I was always respected, listened to and never questioned. The luxury of being spoiled, however, soon became nothing but a boring experience, a comfortless **ennui**, and I would often wonder whether Danny had a more satisfying life amid the constant **turmoil**.

But no matter how different our family lives were, Danny and I blended together and functioned in **singular** unity, **redeeming** one another's weaknesses with our strengths while fulfilling our own wants and desires. Danny **goaded** and **impelled** me to break free from a life of **blasé complacency**, while I provided him with approval, support and reassurance that he found **wanting** in his own life.

The seventh grade marked new developments both in our relationship and in pranking. I found myself more actively involved in sports, while the new year **afforded** Danny new opportunities to add to his **repertoire** of pranks. Pranking had now become for him a means to get even with others, to **assert** his power and make others fear him.

As we entered Saint Paul School, we were ready to challenge new and unfamiliar surroundings. The high school students had also experienced recent changes, for this was only the third year in which the school had expanded from a four-year high school to a seventh-through-twelfth-grade facility. After 120 years of tradition, Saint Paul opened its doors to allow more students and more funds towards a bigger and brighter future. The faculty were **novices** when it came to handling the **temperaments** of junior high schoolers like Danny, and by the middle of the seventh grade Danny was well-regarded as "most likely to be kicked out" before even reaching his freshman year.

I experienced my own problems – which took me away from school for two weeks – but they weren't related to Danny. They **eventuated** from the very thing I loved most: football.

Adults have this mistaken **notion** that winning is everything, but when a fifth grader believes it – and believes it for one-and-a-half years – it becomes more than a "**notion**." To a pre-teen boy **infused** with a "winner-take-all" philosophy, discovering one day that winning isn't possible all the time **imports** more than simply being "mistaken."

The misery of realization for me came swiftly when the *Saint Paul Tigers* faced the *Waikiki Marauders* for the seventh grade jayvee football championship. We clung on to a 7-3 lead but saw it slip away in the final minute of the fourth quarter. Their quarterback, Sam Kahanu, **executed** a perfect quarterback-sneak, flying past me as he hurtled into the end-zone. I was right there to meet him, ready to ram him back to Waikiki, when I was suddenly sandwiched between two Marauder monsters. The lights went out just as Kahanu passed by.

Two days later I awoke at nearby *Kaiser Medical Center* suffering from what was **euphemistically** termed a **cerebral hematoma**. I knew what had happened: I was illegally and mercilessly squashed. My brains had been so badly scrambled that my vision was blurry and I could barely remember my name. But I did notice my friend in the blue corduroy slacks and Saint Paul T-shirt sitting right in front of me, beside my mom and dad. My truest friend hadn't forgotten me. Danny was my real friend – that I perceived clearly – his face ringing a familiarity even stronger than

As we entered Saint Paul School, we were ready to challenge new and unfamiliar surroundings.

my parents'. His image weighed so heavily on my mind that when the doctor came and asked if I could remember my name, I had supposedly answered "Danny" as I fell asleep.

I missed two weeks of school, returning to find little change except the amount of homework I needed to catch up on. Danny visited me at the hospital every day, seven days a week, even if just to drop by and say hello for a few minutes and tell me about his latest pranks.

While I was out of school, Danny had discovered that throwing firecrackers in a stairwell left a more lasting impression on others than simply **filching** candy. People screamed, bolted and generally panicked in ways which we had never before seen. I stared bright-eyed at my friend as he **recounted** the many **escapades** that he and his new-found friend Chip had **collaborated** on in the past few days. The variety was seemingly endless. One weekend, the two hurled water-balloons from atop a parking lot, creating a **mayhem akin** perhaps to the attack on Pearl Harbor.

More adventures followed during my brief absence. The two had become terrors in town, the Waikiki bus drivers coming to **loathe** – and also perhaps fear – the duo as they eventually **emblazoned** graffiti on every seat in the bus. I thought it was just a matter of time before the drivers would begin to kick the **musketeers** off their routes, but for some reason I never clearly understood, Danny and Chip never missed a ride in the months they continued their **vandalous** ways, were never physically removed from a bus, and were hardly more than mildly **reproached** for the **multitude** of **misdeeds perpetrated** upon the buses and toward the **hapless** victims who rode on them. The elderly ladies received the worst show of Aloha spirit, each of the two boys lying down atop the span of the two-person seats rather than affording them the comfort of a place to sit. The two had an answer for every comment, for every request; usually, the communication was short and sweet and **laced** with four-letter **expletives**. Before long, the regular passengers learned to avoid **inciting** or **kindling** a **fracas** by simply standing and hoping that one day the boys would "grow up."

As Danny related the events I missed while I **convalesced**, I could feel the persuasive power in his speech. Every word he said meant more than anything else I could hear, even if it included the name of Chip, a new **rival** for me. Danny was my idol, the better half who was experiencing the world while I lay confined in a hospital bed. And his warmth and understanding, demonstrated simply by visiting me every day, gave me a new perspective on life. It wasn't necessary to win all the time, I realized, as long as a person could have a true friend like Danny to be there when times were tough.

When I finally resumed my normal life of student, Danny seemed to have discovered something new about our friendship. In my need for his help, he in turn found satisfaction being able to offer sincere and **heartfelt** understanding rather than simply be a **conspirator** of pranks. He found meaning and purpose in this new, mature role, and together we gave each other what we each needed most: assistance for me in my homework backlog; meaningfulness in Danny's life, something his mother gave him little of.

21

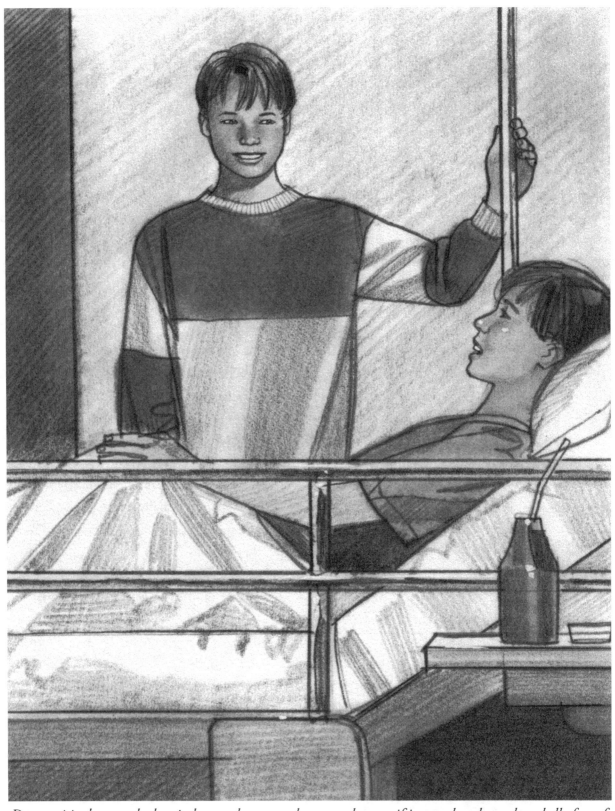

Danny visited me at the hospital every day, seven days a week, even if just to drop by and say hello for a few minutes and tell me about his latest pranks.

The weeks rolled along without any further setbacks for me, though Danny returned to and accelerated his pranking with Chip. But our friendship during my **trying** times had proven itself to be something special, a friendship no one could destroy. Chip was only an acquaintance, whereas I was a friend. I felt secure that it was just a matter of time before Chip would become but a fading memory in Danny's life. I was convinced that nothing would ever separate us.

Then came the summer, and Danny was gone.

CHAPTER V
The "Problem"

I can remember so **vividly** the last day I saw Danny, one week after our seventh-grade school year had ended. The Saint Paul summer carnival took place on Friday and Saturday, and we elected to go together to the final evening's activities. On weekends we usually went to the movies, **conversed** afterwards about anything on our minds, and highlighted the occasion by playing video games until midnight and then strolling through Waikiki en route home. If we **opted** to play basketball instead, we would always be on the same team, contributing to each other's successes and sharing equally in victory or defeat.

On this special weekend at the summer carnival, we feasted on snacks – everything from corn-on-the-cob to cotton candy – and **reveled** in the muddiness of the rain-soaked grounds, feeling **exhilarated** and **unencumbered**, unchained at long last from the **drudgery** of the long school year. I braved the roller coaster while Danny looked on, and then we both dared to ride the *Big Zipper* and the newest ride, the *Gravitron*. The evening **radiated** an **essence** of **ethereal enchantment**, acquaintances we encountered were long-lost buddies, and I felt it was a time I would **cherish** for weeks and months to come.

The next morning, Danny wasn't home. The words of truth attacked my senses through the phone lines.

"No, Danny went to Maui with Chip. He didn't tell you? Just like him, too lazy to tell anyone anything." His mother had few if any good words to say about him. It was as if she found pleasure in misery, as though every negative comment would earn her a better standing in the eyes of the world.

"No, he didn't say anything to me about it."

"I should have know better. I give him too many good things. I spoil him, that's what I do. Taking a trip and nobody knows. Next time, I'll know better. Wait 'til he comes home. He'll remember this trip–"

"But I'm not angry with him, Mrs. Oakley, I just was surprised that he–"

"It doesn't matter. He has no respect, no responsibility. Wait 'til he gets home. He won't forget this lesson."

I had to hang up quickly – I couldn't follow her **rationale**. Danny had undertaken a **clandestine** adventure with Chip; all I did was call to find out where he was, and suddenly he was being **lambasted** for doing something, or for not doing something – I really didn't know which.

My final words to his mom must have sounded alien, for all I can remember saying was "Tell him I said 'hello'."

I was lost. Everything grew hazy, and I could feel myself in the roller coaster chasing an image I couldn't catch. Chip was in the next car, but he was always ahead of me. He was on the winning side. He was Sam Kahanu come back to haunt me.

The flashback to that **debilitating** game was too much for me. Something snapped inside and all I could see were objects flying in the air, a telephone crashing against the chandelier, pencils and books and papers all flying wildly about. I had lost control. I had lost a friend. I had lost. Again.

☆ ☆

The next few weeks were **muddled**. Danny returned, but I couldn't remember whether he phoned me or not. I had re-entered *Kaiser Medical Center* for observations and possible **hematoma** complications but then was advised by my doctor to seek a psychiatrist. I didn't resist the counseling. In fact I rather welcomed it, afraid that something deep inside was triggering these explosions at will, beyond my conscious control. I needed to know the source of the problem and the way to help **defuse** the ticking bomb.

His name was George Wong. That's the first thing I noticed as I entered his office. "George Wong, M.D." in solid black letters. He was a real doctor, or a pretty good prankster. When we first met, I knew he was for real.

"Jeremy, I've read about your problem. Can we call it a problem?"

"Call it what you like. I want to know what you have to say about it."

"I'm not sure I can say much, because it's your problem. But if we can get it out into the open, maybe we can help find some solutions together."

I'd watched enough episodes of *Who's The Boss* and *Roseanne* to be **wary** of **superficial** chatter trying to pass for **solicitous** regard. "How much do you get paid to help me solve 'our' problem?" I wasn't about to become some **sniveling lunatic** confessing his sins to a paid assassin.

"It's your problem, not 'our' problem. The solution may be ours, but the problem is yours. And it is a problem, isn't it? Or is it all right to lose control over as minor a thing as a friend?"

The **perspicacious** psychiatrist had exposed a sensitive nerve, and I knew we had much to learn about one another. I didn't wait a moment to inform him of my true feelings about friendship. "Don't talk about Danny like that. He's more of a friend to me than you can ever guess." My blood began to boil, and I felt the flashes of haze returning.

He was a real doctor, or a pretty good prankster.

"Danny, so that's his name. I didn't think you'd have reacted as you did to a matter of schoolwork. It had to be over a friend. So his name is Danny. Okay, I see your point. No reason to get defensive. I was wrong, I admit that. So now where do we stand?"

The **candor**, the **immediacy** of his admitting being wrong took me off guard. The fuse stopped burning and I regained my composure. He had understood my feelings, and I began then to accept him as a person truly interested in what I had to say.

We saw each other every Tuesday and Thursday for an hour, as I desperately tried to find the source of my problem. But in all the meetings, despite all the **frankness** in relating to the doctor my football experiences and my **collaboration** with Danny and with pranking, I never once mentioned the name of my true competitor, the one I knew I could never defeat on equal grounds. I sensed the situation but could not own up to the realization that Chip would be a part of my life just as he was part of Danny's. I had to learn to live with it, but I could not accept the fact.

Dr. Wong became my friend and counselor during the summer months when I didn't see Danny. I concentrated more and more on my reading and on my writing, filling pages upon pages of personal expression from poetry to drama. I discovered a great love for early British writers such as Chaucer and Shakespeare. The romantic and **chivalric** days of Sir Gawain and later of King Arthur, and the **lineage** of the Henry kings led me away from the problems I had and unlocked the doors to distant fantasy-lands inhabited by magicians and sorcerers and princes and **fair maidens**. I brought along my stories to Dr. Wong, showing a side to him that I shared with no one else, not even Danny.

Then came the bomb, that **devastating confrontation** with the naked truth. It was a quick return to hell, a piercing blow that had effects far beyond what I would have ever suspected. My silence had masked the **profound** nature of my torture, and when the truth was cast **brusquely** upon me, the bomb exploded, **disintegrating** every word I might have defended myself with.

One week before school was to begin, I was scheduled for my final meeting with Dr. Wong. I had managed to convince everyone, even myself, that I would never again need to worry about losing my temper and losing control of my actions.

As I entered the office, confidence guided my words. "Well, this is it, huh Doctor? I seem to have passed every test you've thrown at me, right?"

The psychiatrist looked out the window, gazing upon the streets of Honolulu which lay seven stories below. I could feel something change in the room, some mysterious **aura** now **hovering** about me, exposing a hidden secret. "Do you think so, Jeremy?" he asked calmly. "Do you think I should say you're completely well and healthy and capable of going back to school, back with all your friends?"

I looked at him **addled**, fearing something I could not identify. "Did I do something wrong?" I **queried solemnly**. "Maybe I shouldn't have told you about my pranks."

27

"No, Jeremy, what you've told me is between you and me. There's not a thing you've said that I can argue with or condemn you for."

There was a pause of seemingly infinite length. I broke the silence. "What then? What?"

"How about Chip?"

The truth was out. He knew the whole story, or at least enough to show that I hadn't come clean with him. All the weeks we were friends I had left out one important detail, and it singlehandedly **undermined** whatever friendship we had built. Chip had again destroyed my efforts. Again. Again. Again! The fuse relit and the violent explosions **ensued**.

CHAPTER VI
Compromising Friendship

I missed the first three weeks of the eighth grade, undergoing instead **intensive** counseling at the *Hilo Rehabilitation Center*, a special hospital which served both as a counseling center and a **sanatorium**. Since it was located on another island, I was spared the embarrassment of having anyone accidentally discover my whereabouts during that time. I had simply "taken a vacation," and two hundred miles of ocean lay between me and those who could identify me.

When I returned to Saint Paul I felt more secure, more confident that I could at least accept compromise, if not defeat. Rather than having winners and losers, life was presented at the Center as a series of events in which everyone compromised, some more than others. So-called "winners" were simply those whom the compromise favored moreso than the so-called "losers," a balance that shifted from one side to the other during the **vicissitudes** of life. We were thus all winners and losers mixed together – or as was more **compatible** with Center objectives, we learned to consider ourselves fortunate to be exposed to both sides of compromise, no matter whom it favored. In fact, every failure was interpreted as a new experience more valuable than any single victory we might ever **attain**. We learned to gain from our experiences, not suffer from our defeats.

The new perspectives presented at the Center helped me regain a positive attitude toward myself, no longer seeking to hide from Danny's friends but instead **readily** accepting their presence with **subdued acquiescence** rather than **manifest animosity**. This concept of compromise did not, however, **quell** my desire to seek Danny's attention, despite the fact that his relationship with Chip had **flourished** through the summer and into the beginning of the school year. Although I had suffered the mental strain from the competition which silently grew between me and Chip – a silent monster that nearly destroyed me during the summer – out of this **harrowing** summertime experience came a strength and determination to move in closer and regain the **amity** I had shared with Danny before Chip took over my function.

When I first approached Danny in chapel upon my return to school, he reacted as though we had just seen each other the day before. The words made me feel all the more confident that I could overcome the jealousy which sprang out from competition.

"Did you get all your homework assignments?" he asked me casually and in his usual socially distant manner. "Mrs. Kaschewicz said you'd be back this week, so I saved all my papers in case you'd need any answers." Danny's concern for me had not **waned**; he was simply trying to **curb** his enthusiasm while in the company of his **peers**. It wasn't necessary for us to discuss his summer with Chip or my affairs that had separated us over the past weeks; we were together, we were still friends. I only hoped we would continue to remain close friends without having another summer, or another person, come between us.

The first quarter of the eighth-grade school year indeed provided me with the perfect opportunity to get closer to my best friend, three developments helping me shift the advantage to my side, away from my **rival**. They were **discrete** developments, but together they provided a **synergistic potency** that **ensured** my reinstatement as Danny's right-hand man.

My **acquisition** of a lifelike Mini-Uzi at a most **fortuitous** period helped **rekindle** Danny's interest in my **exploits**. *Rambo* and *The Liquidator* were hot, artillery was the "in" thing and the Mini-Uzi machine-gun had gained the reputation of being the most "rad" hardware on the market. It wasn't enough to have a weapon that could kill; we needed one that could almost literally "blow them away." The Mini-Uzi fit the description perfectly, and I was the first on my block to get one.

Walking into a store or down Waikiki carrying a **sophisticated** piece like the Mini was like driving down the street in a *Lamborghini*. People noticed. Boy did they notice! Maybe it brought back memories of their war days, or maybe they just feared what they weren't certain was a toy, but boy did they react. We had power, more than water balloons could ever offer. My weapon became Danny's, and I **relegated** myself quite willingly to be his **adjutant**. He became my protector.

A second change which helped bring us closer together was entirely of my own design. I noticed that from the day we began our consistent decline in **academic** excellence, Danny was getting hassled by his mom.

"Danny, you bring home such poor grades. Bad boy. I pay four thousand dollars for one year and you get bad grades. You don't study, you don't care. Why should I keep you in private school? You are lazy, like your father. I want you to study hard or you don't go back next year. And don't hang around those bad boys who don't study. I want you to be smart. You are so lazy, so lazy like your father. I don't know what to do with you."

I knew then and there I needed to help Danny, to keep him at Saint Paul and to **befriend** his mom with a show of **academic prowess**. Even though we took different classes, I worked **sedulously** to repair his **scholastic** standing. Within three quarters, his grades had climbed from F's and D's to B's and C's. In the meanwhile, mine **plummeted**, saved only by Danny's heroism and **cunning** strategy at year-end in Mrs. Kilbraith's house. I knew from then on that I would need to work hard for both of us, keeping Danny in Saint Paul and proving myself a good academic influence in the eyes of his mother. I never flunked another class again – with or without **alterations** – and managed to pick up a great love for reading and writing in the process.

The third factor which changed Danny's relationship with Chip was Sarah. Words hardly describe the **seraphic pulchritude** and **angelic** innocence Sarah possessed. Her golden hair flowed breast-length, covering the femininity which had yet to **effloresce**, an **incipient** bloom reserved from view as though a budding flower waiting to one day be plucked and treasured forevermore by that special someone. And Danny seemed destined to be the prince of fortune.

I was with Danny when he first met Sarah. On a warm Saturday afternoon in mid-November we were together at the *Fun Factory* in Waikiki, **engrossed** in *Space Warriors* – one of the series of new

I was with Danny when he first met Sarah.

3-D video games imported and displayed for the visitors to drop their quarters into and participate in a **metaphysical metamorphosis** alongside **anthropomorphic androids** engaging alien **entities** in an **eclectic array** of absorbing adventures. Danny was seated atop the custom-made video-stool, guiding his troops while I entertained myself with a new, updated version of *Asteroids*.

As the **galactic onslaught** progressed, I suddenly **envisioned** what looked to be *Snow White* **lithely** passing through the land of space monsters, then realizing she was no vision but a mirror-reflection appearing on the glass. Sarah glided slowly past as though **vested** with **gossamer** wings, then gazed our way as though an angel **infusing** us with inspiration, silently **exhorting** us to continue in our chosen **crusades**. The **ambience** assumed an **ethereal resplendence** for a split-second, until Chip unexpectedly shattered the **empyreal** atmosphere by entering the video parlor and engaging Danny in **tactlessly jejune** conversation quite **unbecoming** in the presence of such **divine grace** and **sylphic splendor**. His **puerile prattle** was **anathema** in the sacred **pantheon** of the **pristine** princess, and Sarah could not help but find the **slew** of words passing her **undefiled** ears to be **crudely offensive**.

"Cool it, Chip," Danny growled **menacingly** through the corner of his mouth. He was obviously as aware of Sarah's presence as I was, and I knew a showdown was **imminent**.

"Why, what's the matter? You getting turned on by the people here?" Chip sensed the competition, but I **intuitively** knew he had already lost. Chip was about to put his friendship with Danny on the line, and I stood by quietly and confidently for the fireworks to begin.

"Chip, shove off. I don't need your wise remarks." Danny then stopped playing, spun around in his chair and stood up, facing Chip squarely, their height and slim figures matching almost as though they had come from the same pod. Danny's voice had turned icily cold.

"All right, I catch your drift. Danny's bad, huh? Oh yeah, really bad now. Yeah, watch the girls run to him, 'cause he's bad. Sure Danny, sure. You're just too bad for me." The words meant nothing. Chip couldn't compete with such **splendor**, such **immaculate** and **impeccable irreproachability**, such silent **celestial comeliness**, and the words just trailed off into the corridors of **oblivion** as he walked away with his tail between his legs. He had been rejected, but it wasn't the end of the world for him. Chip was **hardy** and **resilient**; he'd bounce back quickly. But the moment offered me the chance to be Number One, and I **gloated** over the **serendipitous** circumstances that had led to my good fortune.

✩ ✩

Sarah became Danny's closest and only female friend. She offered him something I could never provide. She became his sister, his mother and his guiding light. As the second quarter of school approached, Danny began to show new **vitality** and direction, seeking a more mature path rather than adding to his inventory of silly **antics**. I initially had mixed emotions as to whether the relationship between Danny and Sarah would help or hurt my friendship with him, notably afraid that one ill-timed event or poorly chosen word on my part regarding Sarah might **jeopardize** or even **summarily terminate** our friendship just as quickly as one incident seemed to have spelled the doom of his friendship with Chip.

Quite the opposite happened. My friendship with Danny grew more intense alongside his deep devotion for Sarah. When together, the two were **virtually** inseparable, and though they had no classes together – Sarah was only in the seventh grade – the good fortune that they both attended the same school **secured** the **propinquity** necessary to **nourish** a growing and **enduring** relationship. In the few moments shared with Sarah during school, Danny's restless youthful passions were **slaked**, and his telephone call to her in the evening **sustained** his **uplifted** spirits until the next day would once more bring them together.

Meanwhile, my activities with Danny enjoyed a **renaissance**. We were back together – at long last – and no matter what Danny did, no matter whom else he would spend his time with, I knew I could accept it. I knew I could control myself.

It took me three months – three long months of accepting compromise as the governing principle in life – to bring the scales closer towards me. Not win or lose but by compromised advantages in small doses, I gained Danny's favor once more. The Mini-Uzi, my **academic** value and Sarah all brought me closer to Danny in the first half of the eighth grade. And with Sarah, Danny found a peace he had never before experienced: a simple, innocent love affair filled with **visionary** dreams and untold thoughts. It was the type of relationship one could only describe as 'virgin puppy love,' **encompassing** all the **unpolluted** and unquestioned ideals that only two children can imagine. There were no problems, only **resolutions**; no questions, only blind commitments; no compromise, only undying surrender.

I felt that an enlightened spirit had **enraptured** him, **whisking** him away from his **wayward transgressions** and **habituating** him to a **virtuous** path of **righteousness**. With his new **beatific beacon** there to **emblazon** his road to **redemption**, I thought his days of pranking had become **passé**. I couldn't have been more mistaken. Danny had instead discovered, midway through the eighth grade, the most dangerous **justification** for pranking and became the number one **juvenile** suspect on all the Waikiki police reports. Danny had rededicated his **nefarious** activities to Sarah, calling it 'love,' though I could only look upon it as misplaced **chivalry**, a self-destructive **bravado** similar to that displayed by soldiers in behalf of an ideal which they are convinced is worth dying for. For Danny, this devotion to a cause – Sarah – was as real as life itself, and I knew better than to cast it off as some harmless puppy love. There is no such thing as harmless love.

33

CHAPTER VII
The Turning Tide

I think it was during our eighth-grade Christmas holidays that Danny first became a household name for the blue-and-whites patrolling the Waikiki **precinct**. Danny's schooldays had become a **diversionary** escape from home, affording him the freedom to meet Sarah and share dreams that parents didn't understand. He had even written poetry for her:

> *"Your eyes are diamonds that sparkle*
> *against the deep-blue skies of paradise.*
> *The winds whisper your name*
> *and I come following to share when you are there."*

Danny, **extravagant** as he would always be, carved the first line of the **enamored encomium** on the back of one of the desks in her history class, surprising her as only a love-stricken eighth-grader could, letting the world know that his love for her would be etched in eternity.

Nobody suspected the true identity of the poet, no one except Sarah. She had been prepared for some time that her **doting** prince would reveal his **adoration** in a way no one else would dare try. Danny was proud, happy, and daring. Nothing was too good for his prized possession.

☆ ☆

December was an unusually cold and **blustery** month in Hawaii; the **inclement** weather forced us indoors. Our normal after-school activities were **curtailed**, and other than discuss homework or listen to Danny **wax** philosophical over his **fair damsel**, there was little for us to do together. In addition, even though I had worked so hard to become close with Danny – and had succeeded in my **quest** – I found other interests claiming more of my attention and began to distance myself somewhat from him as the holidays neared in favor of perfecting my writing, which **waxed** to fuller **florescence** the more I took out paper and pen.

Danny wasn't mad at me for my leave of absence but looked forward instead to the golden moments of Christmas vacation when he could spend more time with his jewel of the Pacific.

I didn't see Danny very often during the final days of Christmas. I was busy writing and he was busy planning new and bold ways to demonstrate his love for Sarah. But though we had little time together to share our activities, I felt confident that not much could happen to either of us in three weeks.

The Christmas holidays passed all too quickly, and I **yearned** to renew my friendship with my closest **comrade**. I phoned him to wish him a happy new year, but as he spoke I knew something unpleasant had occurred; there was a note of **distress** in his voice.

"What happened, Danny?" I inquired seriously.

"Oh, you wouldn't understand." He wasn't the kind of person who would blurt out the facts without some persuasive **prodding**.

But I knew how to open him up, to loosen his tongue. I'd become expert at uncovering his innermost thoughts and schemes. "I'm your friend, right? And don't friends stick together?"

"Yeah, I guess." Danny was more at ease; we were still true friends. "But I don't want you to get involved. It's between me and Chip."

My blood pressure instantly soared as I heard the four-letter word of my competitor. I was caught unprepared, expecting no less than another **predicament** which we could **collectively resolve**. But Chip **connoted** competition, the one problem I could never before handle. Danny knew why I had missed the first three weeks of my eighth-grade school year, though everyone else thought I had suffered another football injury. The real reason was Chip, my competitor, the threat to my stability. Danny knew I felt **uneasy** about his friendship with Chip; yet, there was little he could do now to prevent the truth from surfacing. He and Chip were together again and had run into some trouble; I had already detected the personal **exigency** in his voice. There was no turning back for either of us. I had to know more.

"I'm going to get those guys, Jeremy," he added with **wrathful indignation**. "I'm going to make them pay for every rotten thing they said to me in front of Sarah." His voice was **tremulous**, bordering on crying. It cracked as he continued. "I was with her and Chip. All we were doing was shopping. We'd planned the whole thing out. It would've worked like a dream. Those bums. Those lousy rotten bums." He paused, catching his uncontrolled breath.

As I listened, I knew the news was far worse for me than for Danny; Chip was no longer a **banished pariah** but instead Danny's welcome **ally**. Their friendship had been **resurrected**, placing me once more on the outside. During the holidays, I had mastered my writing at the expense of losing my closest friend. My eyes began to get misty.

Danny described how the three were involved in a **petty** shoplifting incident which the security officer turned into an **ostentatious** display of **humiliation** by handcuffing the two boys in front of Sarah. Danny's mother was notified and the police were informed of the affair. It was Danny's first serious brush with the law, but it was an event he held the retail store personally responsible for. He was not about to let his **degradation** go **unrequited**, as he now **vented** his **ire** and hinted at a **retaliatory** attack to show the private patrol that it didn't pay to mess with him.

"I don't know how, but I'll get them, every last one of them. Chip and me, we're gonna get 'em back." The words were out and he felt relieved to have **divulged** his intentions. But Danny had unknowingly stripped me of my medals in the process. "No, Jeremy, no need to worry," he continued with surer footing, "I'll get them back. Don't worry."

I couldn't speak. I couldn't react. All I could do was remember my own personal disaster, my own **devastating** tragedy which came hauntingly back to life with the mention of Chip. I thought I might never again feel the **acute** sting of competition, but Danny's words on the telephone inflamed my insecurities and reignited a short fuse. "But I don't want you to get involved. It's between me and Chip" were the final words I heard before I drifted, flashing back to my own **traumatically wrenching** episode five months earlier, back to the worst summer of my life. When I regained my concentration, the voice on the other side of the phone was gone. The line was dead. My **profoundly penetrating** flashback had drawn me out of consciousness for fully a minute; Danny must have felt we had been disconnected.

I hung up the phone slowly and softly, allowing my blood pressure time to return to normal. The explosions hadn't **recurred**, and I discovered I could handle the problem better than before. My initial feeling was wrong; I wasn't losing my grip again. I had subconsciously learned to accept that there are no absolutes, no winners and losers, but simply those who have benefitted from advantages resulting from compromises. Those violent explosions would never **plague** me again. I breathed heavily and regained my **equanimity**. I felt relaxed. A calm inner peace came over me as I realized it was never too late to come back – I would have the opportunity to turn the tide in my direction once more, little by little.

CHAPTER VIII
A New Year's Scheme

Three days later, New Year's vacation was over and school resumed; students and teachers recovered from the excitement of the holidays and began counting down the school days until summer. I never realized how much the faculty also **pined** for the **solace** of summertime until I spoke with Mr. Osmar, Danny's British Literature teacher. The **discourse** began formally but turned out to be a rather **convivial**, informal chat. I remember the traditional opening lines. "Good morning, sir. I hope you had a pleasant and restful holiday."

"Thanks Jeremy," the teacher replied with enthusiasm. "Now how many days do we have until summer?"

"Well, I really haven't counted, sir. Are you planning to teach classes during the summer?"

My ignorance fascinated him. "Sure, and I also teach when I go home. In fact, I don't sleep at night; I simply teach people how to study around the clock." He looked right into my eyes, serious as the first day I walked by his class and heard him recite the school rules to the class. Then a small grin began to build from one corner of his mouth, spreading its **infectious** good humor and bursting from within a laughter I thought adults had forgotten. The image of being a twenty-four-hour-a-day teacher was so **novel**, such a sign of student innocence that he could not maintain his professional **countenance**. His deep brown eyes watered as he leaned over and rested one hand upon my shoulder. "Jeremy, you're all right. I like your style."

Then I understood what he meant and why it was all so funny; we became good friends from that day on. I was starting the new year on the right foot, making new friends and sharing in new perspectives. Even the teachers seemed to be only grown-up students wishing for the same things as everyone else. It felt great to know that some adults are human, too.

I bumped into Danny while walking home after school, **feigning indifference** though **intent** on working my way closer to his confidence – as things had been before the Christmas holidays separated us. He was the first to speak.

"Mr. J., what do you say?"

"Hi Danny. Long time no see, Mr. D." The words of familiarity rolled off my tongue and sweetened my **palate**. I smiled and waited to hear more from my **inexpugnable** idol.

"What happened on Friday? We were cut off and your phone was busy, so I couldn't get back to you."

"Oh, I don't know. But I heard what happened." I began to formulate my thoughts. "So what are you going to do? Get even?"

"Well, I don't know. I figure that Chip and me could drop some firecrackers when the store's the most crowded, but I know they'd spot us coming a mile away."

"Besides, you could get into a lot of trouble doing that. I mean real trouble."

Danny paused and sat atop a window railing, **perturbed** by my parental guidance. "Mr. J, you're always thinking too much. Danny doesn't get caught. Nobody stops me. I do what I want, and that's what's real. The only trouble is what I make for others. I don't get mad; I get even."

Danny had developed a strange philosophy on **morality**. I could understand pranking when it was for fun, but once it was employed to gain power and take revenge the word took on a more **insidious connotation**. He saw himself as **infallible**, always right and always safe. He hadn't played football.

"Anyway," he continued, "I was hoping that maybe you could help me figure something out. After all, we're friends, right?"

I loved to hear him say that word to me. 'Friend.' There was no finer word in the English language. No one word could mean more than what a friend was for me. The list of associations was endless. Warmth, companionship, dreams, sharing good and bad moments, surfing, movies, ice cream, they all became three-dimensional with a friend. Alone, they were mere **pretenses** to **simulate** having a good time; but the secret ingredient, a friend, **imbued** color and purpose into the events. I was Danny's friend, he was surely mine. It felt good to hear the **affirmation**. It felt good to be alive again.

"Okay Danny, what can I do?" I replied with **zeal**. Although I would normally be **loath** to commit myself to criminal mischief, at that moment, it mattered little if I would become an **accomplice** in Danny's act of **retribution**. If it meant saving a friendship, I'd have done it a hundred times over.

"Well, Jeremy, I'll leave that to you. You got the brains, I got the guts. Together, we can't be stopped. Right?"

"Right, friend." My words produced a mild head-rush for me, an **exhilaration** much like scoring a touchdown. It was final, it was forever. Just a **fleeting** moment in conversation, but a moment etched in my mind for eternity. The words, the feelings were meant for the stars to hear. The phrase would go down in history. "Right, friend," first said by Jeremy Stone, twentieth-century writer. Perhaps I was **infallible**, too.

By week's end, we had **devised** a **stratagem** which would help in some small way to **requite** Danny, or at least demonstrate that he would not be shamed and **debased** without eventually **exacting** revenge. Chip didn't bother to join us in our **undertaking**; he was **sufficiently chary** and

"...you could get into a lot of trouble doing that. I mean real trouble."

circumspect not to allow one **mortifying misadventure** at a store **compound** itself to personally **perilous** levels in the course of simply trying to save face. Chip wasn't a **foolhardy** gambler; he was a **staunch** survivor.

Sarah and I would enter *Exotic Gifts* – the scene of the **fracas** – on Sunday morning, carrying with us long steel chains. As we walked through the aisles we would **methodically** fasten a chain on each side, securing it onto the display racks with locks. Within a minute, we could easily walk through, construct five separate links, and walk out before anyone on duty would suspect anything. The customers would think of it as some store event, and by the time they found themselves entrapped between the links, we'd be safe amongst the weekend crowd in Waikiki.

Sarah wasn't very comfortable about the whole idea but allowed herself to be an **abettor** in this **juvenile caper**. The plan was **executed** to perfection, and I was convinced we had **sated** Danny's **vindictive virulence** and **stemmed** any further impulses for additional **retribution**.

Sarah and I would enter Exotic Gifts...

CHAPTER IX
The Unwelcome Association

TWO WOMEN INJURED IN WAIKIKI INCIDENT

Two elderly women were treated for minor injuries after tripping over a concealed chain link at *Exotic Gifts* in Waikiki. Police indicated that the incident may have been the result of an attempt to take revenge against the shop, which has recently stepped up its security in order to reduce shoplifting...

The women, aged 74 and 86, were treated and released at Waikiki Emergency but indicated they would press charges against the owner, Mr. Fred T. Soledad.

An *Exotic Gifts* spokesman refused to comment on the charges, simply saying "We won't cut back on our security and we will hire investigators to find out who was responsible."

The front page newspaper article was received differently by Danny, Sarah and me. To Danny, the exposure was proof that he was stepping up in society, becoming a force to be **reckoned** with. For him, the exposure was thrilling and satisfying.

Sarah didn't react quite so positively. She had never expected such publicized results or that people would get hurt. She was noticeably affected, but in her own forgiving manner Sarah didn't blame either of us for the incident. Whether she felt deep personal guilt from her involvement was never expressed, but she never openly criticized Danny or me for having involved her in the **puerile exploit.**

I reacted very differently to the whole affair. For one, I was the **culprit** directly responsible for what had happened, and if caught I would be answering to a **barrage** of serious charges. I also knew that the security guards would eventually recall the incident with Danny, Chip and Sarah, that it was only a matter of time before the police would be checking up on us. They definitely knew where Danny lived; he was no stranger to anyone who patrolled the Waikiki **precinct.**

Danny reassured me, however, that nothing would happen. "So what if they check us out. So what if they think you were in the store. What does that prove? Did they see you put the chains up? Did they take pictures of it? You're safe, my friend. Nobody messes with us. Nobody."

Nobody except the police. They came knocking on the door the following week, while Danny and I were playing cards in his living room.

"Danny Oakley. Danny Oakley, we'd like to talk with you."

"Oh no," I reacted. I could see the police cars parked outside.

"Don't worry, Mr. J. Remember, they got nothing on us. Nothing."

Danny was right. They asked us a **battery** of questions, **spewed** forth a **litany** of **allegations**, but produced nothing **substantive**. It was obvious to everyone that they wouldn't get a confession, yet just as obvious they wouldn't stop checking on Danny. My presence didn't generate any immediate police reaction, so I knew I wasn't on their most-wanted list. Nobody had tied Sarah and me to the incident; Danny was the sole suspect – **ironically**, the one person who wasn't even there.

And so it was during the second half of our eighth-grade year that Danny and I began our unwelcome association with the police. Wherever Danny went, there was sure to be a blue-and-white nearby. And when we weren't in the vicinity of the police, we could feel some private eye breathing down our necks, hot on our trail.

The **surveillance piqued** Danny's risk-taking fancy. Ripping off candy stores now became more than mere child's play – it meant getting away with a crime right under the police's noses. It didn't matter to him if he **purloined** a water pistol, a knife or a pack of gum. The thrill was the same. Danny emerged victorious and **unscathed**, like a champion surfer riding the largest wave on the North Shore without wiping out.

We survived the remainder of the eighth-grade school year without being busted. As the final weeks came to an end and Mr. Osmar's favorite time approached, Danny and I were together once more, **concocting** the plan that rescued my grades – **beguiling** Linda Kilbraith with **deft** deviousness – **ensuring** that Danny and I would enter high school together. We were friends forever, as in the good-old days of the fifth and sixth grades.

CHAPTER X
Breaking Free

Entering high school might have seemed like entering a new world, but because we were already on the same campus the **rite of passage** was not so **pronounced**. When Clint Hanson asked us if we wanted to join the Striped Panthers, I knew vaguely what he was asking and we **consented** with a general **notion** what we were getting into. Another reason I **acquiesced** was due to the manner of the invitation: Hanson didn't "ask" us; he "told" us. His 6'3" frame of muscle provided adequate reinforcement for persuasion as far as I was concerned, though Danny was not **impressed** by him. Instead, Danny was **intrigued** by the image of the gang itself, and thus we both enlisted as new Panthers to accompany our **initiation** into the world of high school.

Joining the club meant more to me than anything else that could be offered at school, not simply because it enabled me to become one of the "chosen few." More significantly, our entry into the club symbolized the closeness which Danny and I had **attained** after what seemed an endless tug-of-war between me and opposing forces. Danny had become my protector, which he further demonstrated when he later told me he joined the club only because I was accepted.

Gerry Sanders was the **head honcho**. Since the first few days he had entered Saint Paul, everyone knew he was "trouble." The scene in Alexander Theater was but one example of the **brouhaha** he **initiated**. Where there was a school fight, he was around. Where there was vandalism, the destruction bore his mark. He could not be controlled by anyone – not his parents, not the teachers, not the principal. But he was **savvy** enough to avoid becoming **inextricably** tangled with the law; he wasn't stupid.

Danny's selection to the club came personally from Sanders. He'd seen Danny in action and had found much potential in the freshman who had once sworn back at Dean Farheim after school. Few students that age possessed such **temerity**; it took someone without conscience, someone like Sanders and someone like Danny. The Freshman was following in the footsteps of the new president who, fully aware of his limited **tenure** on top, sought a successor eagerly desirous of **perpetuating** the **malevolent** Panther **mystique** for years to come. Danny was indeed his **heir apparent**.

As the weeks rolled along and we attended the first couple of monthly meetings, we began to discover just how **calculating** Sanders was in leaving an impression upon the whole student body. The first month's 'activities' included flattening several teachers' car tires, **surreptitiously detonating** smoke bombs during lunch, and **disseminating** rumors linking the principal to the operation of a house of prostitution. The violence and **defamatory** deeds kept all the Panthers happy, as though they had nothing better to do than **deface** personal property and **besmirch** people's lives. I watched but I did not participate. Were it not for Danny I'd have long **decamped**, but instead I chose to stay, observe from the sidelines and hope he didn't get himself more deeply involved as the year progressed. Perhaps he would even choose to quit the foolishness and **decadence** of the pack of lawless animals.

As the Christmas holidays once again zoomed closer, the Panthers **convened** one final time before year-end. Danny gained center stage as he recalled the humiliation of the year prior.

Sanders was the first to react. "Well, my boy, we can't let them get away with that, can we? I think you owe it to yourself and to us Panthers to show those buzzards what you're really all about. So for the time between meetings, I assign you the task of settling the score for once and for all. Don't get mad; get even. That's our slogan, remember that. No mercy – flush 'em out and stomp on 'em."

Danny rocked back in his seat and smiled. "Yeah," he vocalized **assertively**, dreaming of greater glory than he had ever achieved before. And now he'd have the Striped Panthers at his **disposal**, willing to do any of the dirty work to help him achieve his goals. He had been granted **carte blanche** and **plenipotentiary** power, **indiscriminate** destruction at his fingertips. "Nobody's gonna mess with me. Yeah." His faraway smile sent a shudder through my body; this wasn't the same Danny I had **befriended** years earlier.

I caught up with him on the way out of Miller's Annex. "Danny, what've you got planned? I hope it's not gonna get you into any trouble."

"Don't worry, Jeremy, I know exactly what I'm doing." His reply was so calm, so **unaffected** and so **unwavering** that I knew he was already thinking about the specifics of the scheme and had been planning it for awhile. I then realized for the first time that it was the degrading scene at *Exotic Gifts* that had provided the **impetus** that **impelled** him to join the gang and to seek to remedy the **unwarranted** personal **injustice** and **mortification** inflicted upon him. This was no longer pranking. Pranking was child's play compared to where his thoughts were at now. He was entering the big times, **baited** on by Sanders, and I knew I could not **deter** him from his chosen course.

"Danny, promise to keep me posted? Remember, we're friends."

Danny stopped his **swaggering** stroll and turned to face me squarely. "Jeremy, sometimes a guy's gotta do what he's gotta do. Don't worry about me. I can take care of myself. I've been doing it for almost fifteen years."

Another **tremor** of alarm raced through me as I heard these unfamiliar words, words that might well have been etched on a suicide note. My eyes **welled** up with tears. "Danny, please be careful. Please." I was beside myself, completely overcome by an emotional **compassion reminiscent** of my feelings for him at the hospital, where he offered me 100% when I needed it most. My desire to help him now in any way possible was **reciprocal** but far from **obligatory** or **quid pro quo**. The assistance and the plea for **temperance** came from the deepest, most personal chamber in my heart. I feared the worst and fought to preserve those **cherished** moments we had yet to share while we were still young and innocent.

"Don't worry, little brother. Really, don't worry. I'll take care of myself. I promise." He then walked on – leaving me rooted, **immobile, nonplussed**. In the silent moment, I wished and prayed that he was still in control of his actions, that in a more **lucid** moment he might reconsider his next step. Danny was growing up fast, but I knew deep inside he would rather have remained a kid. The Panthers were claiming a victim.

So much had happened so quickly in the recent past that I now prepared myself for thunder and lightning to strike Danny within weeks, possibly days. Only four short years ago, I had first met Danny. Within two years, we were at Saint Paul, pranking our way into Waikiki and acting like big kids. And even after the horror from the separation during the summer – from which I thought everything would eventually slow down and return to normal – the eighth grade still churned out more activity, changes and daring excitement. With the **emergence** of Sarah and Chip, I had found purpose, a reason to hang around Danny, even if only to stake my allegiance and fight for a bit of the **spoils**. The run-in with the police and the desperate efforts to save my grades added to the **variegated vernal venturousness** a **zest** that kept us young, **spry** and mischievous, just like *Puck*. We were little **sprites immersing** ourselves in **picaresque** playfulness, **dauntlessly** tackling the **multifaceted** and **myriad** ventures life **afforded** us. But we were young, and the adult world granted us the benefit of the doubt. We could **rankle** and **vex** the tourists and **wreak havoc** on the bus because we were young and harmless. The world seemed to turn the other cheek to us when we dealt our childish blows. We were granted the freedom of being kids, of growing up and enjoying the imaginary power that we **wielded**, like young boys playing with paper swords and pretending to be members of the *Knights of the Round Table*.

But the Striped Panthers were not kids. Their games were not childish, not harmless. They didn't issue **idle** threats; they carried them out brutally. The world certainly would not look the other way or even dare to turn their backs to them. And Danny was now one of them, one of the Striped Panthers, a gang of real grown-up **vagabonds** with a **vendetta** against the entire world. The next activity was surely not going to be an **innocuous caper**, and its **reverberations** would be far greater than any I had witnessed before. I was not looking forward to the next few days or weeks. I knew something would soon erupt.

I walked away from Miller's Annex vowing to myself never to return to another meeting but knowing only too well that I owed it to Danny to be there if **adversity befell** him. He was still my friend; I would never let him down.

☆ ☆

The semester progressed with no thunder or fireworks whatsoever. In fact, the period of **quiescence** was so **uneventful** that I found myself digging deeper into studies and even picking up a job to occupy my spare time. I began a newspaper route, which limited the leisure moments spent with Danny and my few other friends. Danny in turn seemed to lean toward other people for support. The Panthers gave him the power-base he thirsted for, while Sarah became an even more **intimate** friend to **confide** in. Fortunately, Sarah and I also grew closer, the two of us discussing school and

Danny was now one of them, one of the Striped Panthers...

other **mutual** interests regularly before class and occasionally afterwards. Mostly, however, we talked about Danny. He was the center of conversation, but for obviously many different reasons.

Meanwhile, three separate **factions** had begun to emerge at Saint Paul, all of them strongly at odds with Danny. One group consisted of a vast number of the student body who feared for the welfare of the school with his presence. He had become the twentieth-century *Nero* at Saint Paul and was avoided like the **plague lest** anyone accidentally rub him the wrong way and **kindle** his **ire** or **provoke** him to **vengeance.**

Many parents also feared his influence upon other students, several pulling their teenagers out of Saint Paul in search of safer ground in the public schools. The principal and the deans **conferred** with one another, but since no **tangible** evidence could be **amassed** against Danny to present a solid case, they had no alternative but to wait silently until the **inevitable** day when the big bomb would explode – hopefully, they commented, while still in Danny's hands.

The most vocal opposition came from the teachers themselves, many of whom had **resigned** themselves to riding the bus home rather than risk more expenses for flat tires than their **meager** salaries could afford. Sanders still ran the club, but Danny willingly took credit for the group's **misdeeds**. He never actually admitted to **perpetrating** the acts of vandalism, but rumors spread quickly and he welcomed his name to be associated with the events. Danny had become the B.M.O.C. – "Bad Man on Campus" – and Sanders watched **discreetly** as Danny made the Panthers the **watchword** of destruction at Saint Paul.

It was during the February P.T.A. meeting that the teachers first began to challenge Danny's rights on campus, requesting his presence at the meeting. Facing a **blatant** refusal by him – a written letter in 'short but sweet' **discourse accentuated** by **terse execrations** and **pejorative appellations** – the teachers presented their case **in absentia**. Little was accomplished other than the creation of the school's first **coalition** established with the **singular** purpose of ridding the campus of one student by whatever means possible.

Because the school had pledged to solve all matters internally – maintaining strict separation between church and state responsibilities – the police were never involved in any activities that occurred on school grounds. Beyond the school borders, however, the patrolmen were just as eager to rid themselves of Danny Oakley.

Danny's plans of **retribution** were merely **inchoate snippets** with limited **efficacy**. Rather than carry out a carefully **crafted** and **intricately executed** plan, he and the Panther mob **resorted** to **prosaic tactics** formerly reserved for teachers; blue-and-whites mysteriously had flat tires and broken antennas, but nothing **sufficiently inventive** to merit front-page headlines as we had **effectuated** the Christmas before. The plans did, however, place Danny as a leader among the

Panthers, newly **vested** with the authority to organize and dispense duties to each of his **vacuous lackeys.**

I was rather pleased, I must admit, at his amateurish and **ineffectual** schemes. He could not get into too much trouble without my inspirational support, so it seemed, and I felt more secure knowing that he had not matured intellectually enough to **mastermind Machiavellian mayhem.** I removed myself from becoming **privy** to his plans, **according** Sarah the sole privilege of serving as his **confidante**; she would, of course, faithfully relay the news to me shortly thereafter.

As the first semester of the ninth grade came to a close, I could sense the anticipation by the teachers as they counted down the days until summer. It seemed funny that they were more anxious to end the school year than I was. I had never considered that they too were in class every weekday, from 8:00 a.m. until 3:00 p.m., probably later, and that they had more work to do than any of their students. I felt somewhat closer to the faculty and more aware of the problem that they had in trying to **inculcate** in their students a **morsel** of unappreciated wisdom, seeking to preserve peace within the **hallowed** walls of the educational establishment, yet also having their own **chaotic** lives to **contend** with. I didn't feel like adding to their problems, and so I chose instead to understand them rather than fight them. School had become a learning experience for me, a **novel** experience that I discovered **emanated** of my own **volition.** I had created for myself an environment **conducive** to learning and had become the **beneficiary** as a result of my own constructive choices.

As our freshman year drew to a close, I continued my friendship with Danny at a slight distance, oftentimes finding out about his efforts through rumors before I actually heard them from Sarah or from Danny himself. The Junior prom was abruptly and **unceremoniously** halted when a vat of grease mysteriously overturned near the entrance, setting fire to the wooden floorboards and forcing everyone to flee through the emergency exits. Fortunately, no one had barred the exits, which otherwise might have produced national headlines of the worst nature. Danny was the number one suspect, but I secretly believed it was the work of Sanders. Danny would have probably tried to seal the exits, whereas Sanders had more survival-sense than to risk a life sentence.

Summer vacation passed quickly, and I acquired a **tawny** Hawaiian tan surfing and enjoying shirtless afternoons. I felt a deep inner **tranquillity** knowing I no longer needed to fear running from the police or **accede** to involvement in schemes **detrimental** to my well-being. I felt totally independent and in control of my activities, spending my days at the beach, earning my evening entertainment money from my newspaper route, and filling my spare moments with paper and pen.

I phoned Danny every day to try to convince him to join me, but his direction had taken him further away from the beach and closer to the streets and the nightlife. Rumors from friends hinted that he was pushing drugs, but as long as he wasn't taking them himself I didn't mind. I hadn't changed my attitude regarding **morality**: whatever happened to other people was their problem, as long as it didn't happen to me or my friends. As long as Danny was safe, I felt secure. He was still my closest friend, and no distance could change this feeling.

By chance I occasionally bumped into Sarah in Waikiki, and she updated me on Danny's latest **endeavors**. In her **sublimely eloquent tactfulness** and consideration, she always took the strictest care not to condemn or **berate** Danny, nor to communicate any **unsubstantiated** rumors.

"Danny's doing well, Jeremy," she informed me in soft whispers. "He's been busy working for a nightclub but never forgets to ask me how you're doing."

Sarah seemed so innocent, so **ingenuous** that I really couldn't tell whether she was aware of Danny's true activities. But one thing I did know: she told me everything she knew about Danny. I was also certain that, had she known of any **illicit** activities involving him, she would have **intervened** to try to persuade him to stop – and Danny would have had to be a fool not to listen to her. But such wasn't the case; she was not aware of anything inappropriate in his lifestyle. To her, rumors about Danny were just that – **unfounded** rumors not worthy of a second thought. She believed in him, and I cannot overstate the degree of **reverence** Danny held for her. I simply never really knew just how much he needed her, not until she moved away.

CHAPTER XI
The New Force

When school admitted us as Sophomores, the **inescapable** first rumor of the new school year spread quickly, like a wildfire through a dry forest: Danny had become the next president of the Striped Panthers. Gerry Sanders had graduated with the blessing of all the faculty, hoping to never see him again as long as they lived. But as one destructive force departed, another came to take its place. Danny was now the B.M.O.C. – "Bad Monster on Campus" – the number one person to stay away from at all costs. Power was his middle name, and he knew it. His fancy threads and dark glasses gave way to torn jeans and a semi-mohawk. Dress-code banned such **attire**, but no one – neither faculty nor student body – raised a voice for enforcement of the rule. Danny was the one exception to all rules. Now everyone was listening to him, everyone except his mom.

"Danny, you walk out of this house with those clothes, you go to public school. I don't waste my breath with you. Understand?"

Danny didn't argue with her. He never did, he never would. She was his commander, and he knew she **wielded** real power, not childish threats. So rather than challenge the **insuperable** family **matriarch**, he **complied** but then changed his clothes before he caught the bus, changing back again before he returned home. On occasion students saw him with both sets of clothes, but only I knew the real story, and I would never share the **inviolable** secret with anyone. I had to keep Danny's image **untarnished**. He always wanted to be "bad," and no true friend would deprive another of living up to his **delusions** of **grandeur**. Danny certainly had never told anyone about my trip to the Center in Hilo, and I had long come to understand that friendship included accepting the other person for what he chose to become, for better or for worse.

It was during our Sophomore year that everything seemed to fall apart all at once, as if the world had made a **concerted** effort to destroy a single human being. The victim was Danny. I witnessed as Danny attempted to recover the ground he had lost yet still retain his own freedom amid a **monolithic** system that passionlessly sought to pull him down. As a Panther Danny acted "bad," but I knew that the **persona** portrayed was not the real Danny I had grown up alongside and shared my earliest fantasies with. I could see through the **flatulent façade**, the **vainglory**, and the assumed **arrogance** which hid the real person, the Danny who had not really changed and would never change.

I tried to maintain close ties with him, staying in his confidence so that he would have at least one loyal **confrere** of the same gender. Sarah provided the loving comfort and appeared willing to stay around him forever, but there were certain times during which he needed me more than Sarah, times when I knew he couldn't confess his problems to anyone but me.

The Panther meetings continued monthly but I slowly **receded** from them, reassuring Danny of my **fidelity** to the group, though **mendaciously** maintaining that a writing club with a conflicting schedule had recently also **initiated** me.

"Danny, you walk out of this house with those clothes, you go to public school."

"Don't worry, sport, I understand where you're coming from. You just keep on doing what you do best, and whenever you need help you see me, okay?" Danny's words seemed to reflect great maturity, as though he were suddenly years older than I, but I sensed only too well his insecurity and his **disquietude** in losing my company at the meetings.

"Thanks, Danny," I replied, **asserting** in reassuring fashion, "but you know I'll see you after the meetings, okay?"

His reply left a huge dent in the pit of my stomach, as his social **veneer** was stripped for a moment of honest friendship. "I'm really glad you'll wait for me, Jeremy. Thanks, friend."

I walked home that afternoon cursing everything that I associated with growing up and with grown-ups. The pressures to grow up had forced Danny to become someone he never wanted to become. And now we were walking in different directions, meeting for perhaps our final time. I could not accept saying goodbye, not when he had so openly and honestly called me his friend, a word he couldn't have used very often in his position as king of the mountain. When you're on top, it's hard to have friends. "Why would *anyone* want to be Number One?" I asked myself bitterly and angrily, reflecting upon my own recent **insatiable** desire to be the best in football. I now knew why the **attainment** of **supremacy** was, at best, a hollow victory. I had discovered the **irrefutable** truth from my meeting with Danny: There is no real personal glory in being on top; there are no friends to share the experience with.

As the Sophomore year developed, I heard few rumors about Danny, as though he was consciously avoiding **inciting** further **chaos** or was at least was not taking foolish credit for such **subversive** activities. For my own part, I **eschewed** anything "Pantheresque," adding to my list of credits a journalistic post on the school newspaper. My classes were challenging; I gained more understanding and respect for many of the teachers, especially those who openly expressed their own **qualms** and **trepidations** to the students. I was fortunate to have gotten Mr. Osmar for Advanced American Literature, and he showed immediate familiarity to me, remembering well our short discussion the prior year. He was a **personable** and easy-going man who enjoyed tennis, basketball and movies. One class day, he offered an open invitation for all his students to meet after the school football game to **partake** in free pizza, provided by him. I attended the festivities with half a dozen **peers**, spending several hours engaged in **illuminating** interpersonal communication, an opportunity rarely **afforded** students during class time. Even Mr. Osmar seemed more like a fellow **compatriot**; he laughed and spoke with us, not at us. We developed a **mutual** understanding and respect I have never experienced with any other teacher in all my years of schooling.

Meanwhile, I managed to make room in my busy schedule to see Danny at least twice a week, to chat with him and listen to his dreams and **aspirations**. Sarah had become a source of his latest inspiration, Danny talking of special plans he would **unveil** on Valentine's Day, fully two months away. But unlike in the past, I did not grow weary of his one-track-mindedness and instead expressed my sincerest interest to hear more of his thoughts and ideas. Talking of Sarah was far safer than thinking of new ways to spread Panther **paranoia**.

The Christmas holiday season came and went, but not without my share of excitement. During the latest school year, I had unlocked new doors and discovered exciting sources for pleasure and learning. The **scholastic** calendar **culminated** with a hiking expedition atop Mount Haleakala on Christmas day with the Writing Club, which I did eventually join shortly after leaving the Panthers. We recorded our many adventures both on film and in words, eager to produce a half-hour video as a **memento** of the **excursion**. The two-week **trek** extended past New Year's, returning us home just in time for school.

On the first day back, I heard the rumor that reawakened mild flashes of rising blood pressure: Chip had been asked to join the Striped Panthers. I had wondered why the **avaricious** Panthers hadn't recruited him earlier but didn't voice my curiosity, grateful instead that Danny and I shared something Chip wasn't part of. But with my gradual disappearance from the meetings and activities of the group, Danny had apparently sought a suitable replacement. Chip was replacing me, but this time I did not suffer the **pangs** of competition. I was not desirous to ever become part of the Panthers again and therefore contented myself to watch from **afar**, though still genuinely interested in maintaining close contact with Danny so we could share in our innermost thoughts – with or without Chip's presence.

As Valentine's Day neared, I discovered the nature of the plans Danny had briefly mentioned earlier. He had purchased a 14-karat gold ring for Sarah, which he would present to her at the same time he would ask her to be his steady girlfriend, a **sophomoric** version of **nuptials**. After two years of being friends, Danny was seeking a more secure relationship. Sarah had become such an **integral** part of his life that he knew he could **ill** afford to lose her comfort, warmth and understanding, and with his bold gesture of commitment he was now **affirming** his pledge of love.

I said nothing of this to Sarah but sensed that she had already heard of the **pubescent** proposal through rumors that are **spawned** and **invariably** sweep through schools with little purpose other than to expose, exploit or **foil**. When I mentioned Valentine's Day to her, she hesitated a moment and then looked away as if to avoid **divulging** the **ineluctable** truth that no one else had yet suspected.

"Well, Jeremy, you see, I'm not sure if Danny's planning to go out with me for Valentine's, but I really don't want for him to..." She looked around, nervously trying to finish her thought, "...to take me too seriously."

She turned and faced me with an expression of **bemused bewilderment**, a cross between **paralytic consternation** and **utter vexation** at the events that had led up to this **climacteric**. "I just don't want him to get hurt, that's all," she blurted out almost **involuntarily**.

"I just don't want him to get hurt, that's all."

I knew she was attempting to **allay** the **percussion** of the **stark**, **baneful** truth, and in her **inimitable** way the message was delivered clearly though in a **subdued**, cushioned manner, blunting the piercing arrows and preparing me for what lay deeper. Yet she never **elaborated**; she simply left the suggestive words to be interpreted howsoever I chose to perceive their meaning. I could not explain it to Danny, for she had not said anything definite; and yet, I knew Valentine's Day would not grant Danny the joy he had been planning and hoping for.

I avoided seeing Danny for the next couple of weeks except to chat casually and briefly. Once his thoughts turned to Sarah, I begged my leave so as not to say anything which might arouse suspicion in him. I did not know exactly what Sarah was **alluding** to – whether she had another boyfriend, was gay or had some disease that prevented her from every getting married or having children. Or maybe she was considering entering the ministry – her angelic innocence well supported this possibility. But if she were entering the ministry, what better goal in life could there be than to try to reform Danny, the student considered most likely to wind up in Hell before graduation.

As the day of **reckoning** came, I avoided both Danny and Sarah as though each were capable of turning the nearest person to stone. I **endeavored** to **conceptualize** the episode that would **eventuate** when the two met. I **envisioned** yelling, screaming, swearing, books being thrown and crowds gathering around while the two carried on like **lunatics** on center-stage. But nothing of the sort happened. I braved the silence and the absence of rumors and approached Danny while he was waiting for the Waikiki bus to take him home. I remained silent, fearful of the **rage** that might accompany the first words from him.

"Hey there, Mr. J. Where've you been? I thought you came down with some writer's disease and disappeared into one of your stories." The words were spoken in a friendly, **sober** manner, leaving me momentarily speechless.

"Sorry, Danny," I replied **mousily**. "I knew you were busy and didn't want to get in your way." The words meant nothing; they simply filled up the space while I awaited the next revealing words from Danny, the **lovelorn Romeo**.

But the words of gloom and doom never emerged. Sarah had either experienced a sudden change of heart, or else Danny's love and devotion for her had left him blind to the **subtle implications** that Sarah may have presented. Or perhaps I had been mistaken all the time; maybe it was all just a dream.

I avoided ever mentioning my suspicions to Danny and soon found that he was **enmeshed** in a more serious **imbroglio**, a **dilemma** that threatened to **undermine** his enrollment at Saint Paul School. Danny's **scholastic** problems were beginning anew. He was on the **verge** of flunking out.

Danny's scholastic problems were beginning anew. He was on the verge of flunking out.

CHAPTER XII
Sizing Up The Situation

The first hint I had of Danny's **tenuous** position **academically** came from Mr. Osmar, who oftentimes **conversed** with me after class and sought to learn more about my relationship with Danny. At the time, I felt he was simply displaying **perfunctory** interest for a former pupil, but he soon **confided** in me that many of the teachers were **collaborating**, eager to rid the school of what he called "a problem." Although these first indications of teacher-rebellion were mentioned to me as early as January, I did not consider them serious threats to Danny, who seemed to be able to overcome any **adversity**. I had begun to believe Danny when he said "Nobody can touch me." But as the rumors began to circulate early in March regarding Danny's **bleak** outlook at Saint Paul, I realized Osmar knew more than he had told me at the time. Perhaps now it was even too late for me to help.

I braved the topic with my teacher the day after the latest rumors reached my ears, anxious to find out just how serious the situation really was for Danny and whether Osmar and I might be able to help save Danny from **expulsion**.

"Jeremy," the mild-mannered teacher began as I stood in front of his large oak desk, "I don't see why you want to help him. He's taken his own course, his own way out, and it doesn't concern you anymore. He's made a name for himself; he's made a fool of himself. You have nothing to do with that and you really have nothing to do with him. He was a good kid once, but things happen. Sometimes people change and don't get back on the right track. Danny's off the track, and he's not coming back. Haven't you seen it yourself? Haven't you kept away from him? Hmmmmm?" Osmar sensed that I wasn't moved or taken by his observations, nor that I had made any move to **disassociate** myself from Danny. He continued, "Even if you still like him, don't you see that you've gone in a different direction? What have you two got in common now? Tell me, I really want to know."

So many questions came so quickly, I felt like punching him and running out the door; that seemed the only appropriate way to respond to the rapid-fire **fusillade** of questions which didn't allow me time to assemble my thoughts, hardly even time to get a word in edgewise. But I didn't lash out; I wouldn't simply run away and pretend that I held the answers in my fists. I stood there in front of the teacher as he sat patiently behind his desk, counting to five before I replied as calmly as I knew how.

"Mr. Osmar, you don't understand the situation. You feel that just because Danny is different, he must necessarily be bad." I gave the teacher the chance to reply.

"I'm not saying he's bad because he's different. I'm simply saying that he has turned his individuality, his creative self, against us, against the school. He's trying to create **anarchy**, trying to be king of the hill. Those are kids' games, but he's not a kid anymore and he's not acting like a kid."

"Danny's off the track, and he's not coming back."

"But maybe nobody understands him. I know his family life and nobody there cares about him. And in school, the teachers seem to be more interested in keeping their classes 'safe' rather than trying to deal with the situation. The world is filled with people like Danny, but nobody wants to accept it or handle it, or appreciate it."

"Appreciate what?" Osmar questioned. "Are we supposed to encourage students to promote **insurrection**, to **taunt** teachers and students and declare that authority has no place in today's society?" Osmar was fighting in behalf of all the morals and **pedagogical ideologies** which he in turn **inculcated** in his students, **tenets** that supposedly promoted freedom but yet only sought, at any cost, to ensure security for himself and **perpetuate** the **sanctity** of the **academic** world. But I knew that his views of safety were **misguided**, that it was too late to cling to **puritan** values in an age of **enlightenment**.

"Mr. Osmar, you think that Danny will just disappear if you kick him out of Saint Paul? Do you think he will be out of your life just because he's in a public school? Do you think he'll ever be out of your life when he gets out of school? And do you think he's the only one like that here, or out there, or anywhere? You think he's the only person in the whole school who is fighting the system, fighting everyone because of something deep down inside that wants to be heard? Look at yourself, sir, look at the kind of person you are. You're not like the other teachers. You have shown me a side of yourself that is different from what I've seen in school before. You're a real person, with real feelings, and you're not afraid to share them with me. You're fighting the system too, and I respect you for that, just like I respect Danny for his feelings and his ways of expressing them. If you don't like his style, try to change it. But don't try to eliminate it. Don't follow the herd of other teachers. They'll never succeed."

The **frank** discussion left its mark on the **bespectacled maverick** teacher. He had been young once, and quite recently. In his eight years as a teacher at Saint Paul, he had stood up for his rights and had faced the Board of Directors to defend what he thought was a **valid** reason for promoting change in policies. Danny was a reflection of who he had once been: an individual. Osmar was now caught in a **crossroads** between supporting the school's **parochial** policies or standing behind this **clarion** call for change. He could no longer stand **ambivalently** on the sidelines and observe; I had **confronted** him squarely with the facts. I wrapped it up as though he was judge and jury. "What's the verdict, sir? Is he guilty or not?"

Osmar took off his wire-rimmed glasses in a slow, **deliberate** manner, **staidly assessing** the matter and **cogitating** his options. I waited, reflecting in satisfaction the manner in which I had addressed the problem, reversed the situation and forced my **interrogator** to answer to the final charges. Osmar looked up at the clock behind me, then addressed my ultimate **query**. "Well, Jeremy, here's another fine mess you've gotten me into." He **tittered** for a moment, but I knew he was **temporizing** to clear the cobwebs that had formed. He couldn't escape to the **sanctuary** of summertime. He was now the teacher, an adult – no longer a kid – stuck in the same **quagmire** as Danny. Would he fight on or give in?

"Okay," he began at long last, "I see your point. But I also know how much is riding against Danny. The faculty isn't going to **yield** an inch, no matter where I stand. Three of his teachers have already told me Danny's an **inveterate incorrigible** – and you know they'll do anything and everything to keep him from passing."

Osmar hadn't taken a position, but he had **confided** in me exactly what Danny was up against. I knew I could count on him to keep me posted, to relate the **status** of Danny's **plight** to stay in school, if indeed Danny chose to stay at all. I needed to confirm whether my best friend was even **tepidly** interested in Saint Paul amid all the rumors seeking to **derogate** and **humiliate** him.

I phoned Danny when I got home, telling my folks that my customers could wait a few minutes for their evening papers; the news wasn't going to change anyway. Danny answered, but I could hear his mom yelling at him from **afar**. She had either been informed of the **deficiencies**, or she simply **thrived** on **vociferous caviling**.

"Danny," I began quietly, "I heard about your grades. Is it true?" Of course I knew that what Mr. Osmar had said was indeed the truth, but I needed to know if Danny had heard the news and if he was taking it seriously.

"Yeah, I heard it. My mom heard it, too. She's got a meeting with the principal tomorrow morning."

"What about your dad?" I didn't regard Danny's mom as the **epitome** of **savoir faire** for creating **detente** and hoped instead that his dad could help ease **hostilities** with the school.

"My dad's going golfing tomorrow. He doesn't want to be bothered. He's always said it's my responsibility to do what I think's right. So he's staying out of this. It's his style."

"What do you think they'll say to your mom?"

"Do I care what they say?"

I echoed his thoughts. "Do you, Danny?"

"I don't know, Jeremy. I think I should, but I just don't know. I don't think I've even got a chance."

He seemed serious enough, so I **probed** the subject further. "If you could make it, I mean if you really could pass, would you try?"

"Yeah, I guess so."

"I mean, would you *really* try? Really. Like maybe put in some time to study and maybe even

"Danny," I began quietly, "I heard about your grades. Is it true?"

cool it with bugging the teachers?" I was searching for some degree of commitment, uncertain whether any reply would necessarily be a carefully considered one.

"Yeah, Jeremy, I want to stay. I've got my club, my friends, Sarah. I don't want to lose them. Sure I want to stay. 'Really'."

His final word **impressed** me. He had listened to my question, had made a firm commitment, and had decided with determination that he wished to stay – he wanted to remain part of the student body of Saint Paul. And yet, I wondered whether I was **prostituting** him by forcing him to decide between **conformity** and **exile**. I offered him no middle ground – no chance to remain himself, individual and free – within the walls of the system. He was being forced to abandon at least some of his own pursuits to remain with his **peers**, just as Mr. Osmar had been forced to do so eight years earlier. I had challenged Osmar to seek greater freedom, but now I was persuading Danny to abandon that same freedom. I felt trapped in a **paradox** of confusion, and yet I accepted what little choice Danny had if he wished to stay afloat.

"I'll help you, Danny, as much as I can. I've had lots of the same teachers you have now, so I can help you with the homework. They won't beat us, Danny. They won't kick us out. You can count on me." I hesitated to add "friend"; we were old enough to know who we were without adding childish reinforcements. But somehow, I wish I could have said it. The word lumped in my throat, and I contented myself having at least said as much as I did.

The next morning, I caught up with Danny as he headed for his first class. "How did it go with your mom, Danny?"

He reduced his steady pace, replying in a **subdued** and **solemn** manner. "She's really mad at me. I don't know what she'll do." I noticed that Danny was wearing regular school clothes, his mother being on campus today. "I think she's gonna ground me for a month and I won't be able to see anyone."

"What about me? We've got to work on your homework together."

Danny slowed his pace to a crawl. "She's kind of funny, you know, Jeremy. She probably won't even let you help me with my homework. You know she's done that before."

"Yeah, but what'll that accomplish if you can't figure out what to do? If she's trying to help, it doesn't make sense to keep you stuck inside the house and away from me."

"Does life always make sense, Jeremy?" He stepped up his walk and headed towards the Art building. "I'll try, Jeremy. I'll do what I can, even if we have to work during lunch."

"Can I call you? We could do it over the phone, maybe?"

"You know my mom, Jeremy. What do you think?"

I didn't need to answer. We would be fighting together against the whole world. But we would fight together, just as in the good old days. "Don't worry, Danny, I won't let you down," I called out as our **divergent** steps drew us farther apart. I then turned and headed for math class with a renewed confidence and **resolve**. We were together again, just like kids.

CHAPTER XIII
Changes

"You are no good. Never listen to nobody. Just play, play play." His mom was on the war-path. "I talked with three teachers and they all say you are bad in class, bad, bad, bad. What do I do with you? Why do I have a boy like you?" She was not asking for a reply. This was a one-way conversation, and Danny had no choice but to listen. "I don't want you to go back to that school next year. The teachers they don't want you. Just play, play, play." And with the **vituperation** complete, Danny's mom shook her head and marched out of the kitchen.

I was on the phone with Danny a few minutes later, confirming what I had suspected. "So you're grounded? How long?"

"The way she sounded," Danny chuckled nervously and in a barely **audible** tone, "I'd say for life." His lightheartedly humorous reply reflected relief now that his mom had finished **besieging** him with **disparagement**. With her **invective** behind him, he could move on and once again build from the ground up.

"What do we do now?" I inquired, anxious to begin reconstruction with whatever **implements** and resources were available.

"We've gotta wait. I can't do anything yet. She's threatening to put me in a public high school." He then **recounted** the details of the conversation.

"Don't think about that, Danny," I reassured him. "The game ain't over 'til it's over, remember that."

"Yeah, but then what?"

No one had ever asked me that question. To me, the one-liner meant that things were never over. But Danny, the realist, was considering the what-ifs, and I needed to come up with an answer from my vast **repertoire** of **roseate repartee**.

"Well, after it's over, we celebrate, that's what!" I'd come up with more hope, more **sanguine sustenance**. The sparkle of humor found its way into Danny's heart, returning us to common understanding **redolent** of years past.

"Okay, Mr. J., and I'll bring the popcorn."

"Right on, big bad Danny Brown." The telephone conversation ended in high spirits.

✩ ✩

The seriousness of the situation resurfaced the following day in school, with rumors of a **coup** developing from within the Striped Panthers. One of the newest members was staking his claim at the title of president, if Danny was indeed expelled from Saint Paul. With the smell of **putrescent** meat, the pack was hungry for change – **fealty** wasn't a **prerequisite** for club entrance.

I approached Danny during lunch as he and Sarah were discussing what seemed to be of great interest to both. Perhaps they were **mulling** over the rumors or planning a strategy to bail him out of the **dilemma**. A **pang** of jealousy came over me – would they try to solve the problem without me? I needed to find out what was happening.

"Hi Sarah. Danny, what's cooking?" I **endeavored** to appear only casually interested, placing one hand in my pocket while the other remained wrapped tightly around three textbooks.

"Oh, nothing important, Danny. Just something between Sarah and me."

"Can I help? Has it got anything to do with your grades?" My questions **belied** the **intensity** of my curiosity; I **dreaded** the reply, fearing it would spell the doom of my friendship with Danny.

"No, Mr. J., you're the only person who can help me with homework and that stuff. Nobody'll ever replace you on that, guaranteed."

My **apprehension** was **quelled**; I was still securely part of Danny's plan for recovery. The conversation with Sarah no longer carried with it anything of **import** to me – it didn't affect my position with Danny. I bid **adieu** and started to walk away.

"You know who's trying to replace me?" Danny added as I was leaving.

"No, I didn't really know that anyone was thinking about it."

"Chip."

So the rumors were true, and to add insult to allegiance, it was Danny's own **protégé** who was trying to **subvert** his authority. "I guess a panther never changes his stripes," I replied. "Come to think of it, a panther doesn't even have stripes; he's got spots."

"Dumb name, huh Jeremy?" I could see that Danny was tired of the entire **farcical** club.

"Don't worry, Danny. We'll make it. With or without the others." My words were final and determined. I would let nothing stop me from defending Danny. Not now, not ever.

☆ ☆

The next couple of weeks dragged slowly along, each day drawing Danny **inexorably** closer to his day of judgment – a day destined to yield a guilty verdict despite our most **earnest** efforts to seek **redemption**. Because of restrictions placed upon Danny by his mom, I was unable to personally help him with his homework after school and thus found our **problematical plight compounded** by limited **access**. The **bleak** future seemed hopelessly unalterable until one morning, with but one month of school remaining, a **glimmer** of hope finally sparkled for us. Danny came running after me between classes as I paused to get a drink of water.

"My mom says you can help me. She finally changed her mind, Jeremy."

"You mean we don't need to sneak those phone calls anymore?", I sighed in relief, recalling how the past many evenings had been an exercise in **futility**, trying to explain concepts over the phone whenever his mom was in the bathroom or at work. His dad posed no problem, though neither was he any help in our **industrious enterprise**. He just sat back, watching television and life pass him by, while I meanwhile strove with all my might to withstand the forces that seek to **repress** individuality and mold its members into **mindless minions** of **mediocrity**. Through **stealthy** and **surreptitious machinations**, I braved the **tempestuous** waters and managed to assist Danny to a minimal degree to improve his latest scores, though even my best efforts still didn't produce overall passing grades. Now, however, the seas would be calmer, and the news couldn't have come at a more **timely** and **auspicious** moment.

"That's great, Danny," I continued **optimistically**, knowing that we could now pursue a more dependable plan of attack than through our **tedious** telephone **trysts**. "I'll be over as soon as I finish my paper route. You want to help me?"

"Nah," the president replied with an **affected air** of nobility, "how would it look if people saw me?"

"I think it would look like you're working. What's wrong with that?" I **queried**, shrugging my shoulders to see if he would react to a common-sense **justification** for doing something.

"Thanks but no thanks. I think I'll check out Waikiki 'til you're done." He was still the same Danny I'd known for years – a **trifle indolent**, but charmingly so.

I felt **compelled** to **impugn** his **rationale** for laziness. "Money for nothing, chicks for free, huh Danny?"

"You do it your way, I'll do it mine. **Savvy, comrade?**"

Same old Danny.

With but one month of school remaining... Danny came running after me between classes...

CHAPTER XIV
A Learning Experience

I completed the paper route at 5:30 and rode my bike over to Danny's house, where he was already waiting for me. He was eager to get to work; I hadn't seen him on time like this for anything except the Panther meetings. Perhaps he had established a new set of priorities.

At long last, I was able to help Danny in a one-to-one, **vis-à-vis** spirit of fellowship, no longer limited to long-distance stolen moments and after-lunch **rendezvous**. The work now lay before us and we **coalesced** forces to do battle with the **copious** and challenging coursework. It was Danny and I against the books, against the assignments, against everything the teachers of Saint Paul could hurl at us.

"Where do we start, Mr. J.?" Danny began.

"We start at the beginning. Right from the first part that confuses you. Algebra, that's first." I wanted him to call me "Jeremy," not "Mr. J.," but I **refrained** from sounding like a teacher. What mattered most was the task of learning, not the **obligatory pedantic propriety** that teachers demand from their **servile** subjects. I flashed momentarily upon Mr. Sanchez' class, **steeped** in rules, regulations and formats. And I remembered being **docked** ten points on a quiz because I wrote "1X" instead of "X." And when I asked him the difference between the two, he provided the age-old **stock** reply, "It's the difference between right and wrong: I'm right, you're wrong." The answer produced for me no positive impression, despite Mr. Sanchez' accompanying **sinister** gurgle. He thought he was being funny; I thought he was supposed to be teaching me something.

"Okay, Danny, here's the problem:"

$$6 (X-3) = 4 (X+4)$$

"Now remember, Danny, you've got to expand, then move the variables to one side and the numerals to the other." I was trying to sound official.

"The what? What's a 'variable'? Sounds like a bird." Danny was amusing himself while masking his ignorance.

"Okay, you ham. I'll say it so even you can understand. Comprende?"

"Yeah, 'comprende,' **mein kapitain**."

"Okay, you tear apart those parentheses, throw the letters on one side and the numbers on the other side."

"Like this?" and Danny began to work out the problem in his typical **haphazard** step-skipping fashion.

$$6 (X\text{-}3) = 4 (X+4)$$
$$6X\text{-}3 = 4X+4$$
$$10X = 7$$
$$X = 1\ 3/7$$

"Great, Danny, you managed to get every step wrong. Are you sure you know anything about this stuff?" I glared at him **dubiously**.

"Gee, if I did, Beaver, why would I be asking you for help?"

"Okay 'Wally,'" I **retorted**, following Danny's *Leave It To Beaver* script, "I'll step through this one just for you, big brother, and you remember it for ever and ever."

"Gee, thanks Beave." The dialogue was friendly but I could see we were going 'no place fast,' as the *Three Stooges* had **adeptly** phrased such hopeless situations.

"Okay, Danny, here it is," and I **commenced** writing down in step-by-step fashion the clearest way I knew how to solve the **rudimentary** algebraic equation.

$$6 (X\text{-}3) = 4 (X+4)$$
$$6X - 18 = 4X + 16$$
$$6X - 18 + 18 = 4X + 16 + 18$$
$$6X - 4X = 4X - 4X + 34$$
$$2X = {}^{+}34$$
$$X = {}^{+}17$$

I looked up from my writing, proud of the simplicity and ease with which I had explained the problem. But Danny was evidently bored, gazing instead outside his bedroom window and in the direction of Waikiki.

"I wonder what the surf's like, Mr. J.?" he asked distantly.

"Danny," I reacted with irritation, "how are you ever going to learn this stuff if you don't listen and pay attention?"

"Easy," Danny replied. "You do the work, I get the credit." He had obviously already planned it this way, always one step ahead of the rest when it came to shortcuts.

"Danny," I began, "That won't work. Even if I did help you cheat on your homework, you'd still have to take the tests yourself, and where would that get you?"

Danny was noticeably **irked** by my mention of 'cheating.' His eyes flashed towards mine. "You're calling me a cheater?"

"No, Danny, that's not what I meant," clearly lying through my clenched teeth to preserve a friendship that seemed so close to **teetering** on the edge. "What I mean is that I want you to pass, I want to do everything I can to help you learn the stuff so you can show the teachers what you know." I didn't want to risk the **residual** fallout of the **faux pas**, adding "and I didn't mean to use that word. I'm sorry for even saying it."

Danny was **appeased**, although I doubted that he had changed his plans. He still wanted me to help him cheat.

"Okay, here's another problem, a lot easier than the first one:"

Simplify: 6 x 3 - 2 x 2.

"Okay, now what do you do?" I asked calmly.

Danny had the immediate reply. "I wait for you to tell me."

I threw up my hands in frustration. "Where are we going, man? We're not getting anywhere." I was clearly annoyed and could **foresee** a potential **confrontation looming** in the not-too-distant future. It was only a matter of moments before our period of **reckoning**, our showdown, would have descended upon us. I therefore elected instead to **forgo** math and focus on American literature.

"Danny, I know Mrs. Leopold wants to see you out of Saint Paul, but I think we can ace her test and make her eat her words."

"Okay boss, lay it on me." Danny readied himself for the **didactic** discussion.

I tested the waters, however, before plunging **headlong** into Poe. "Danny, are you really going to listen to this stuff? I mean, I don't want to waste your time if it isn't gonna stick." I had the *Explorations in Literature* book turned to page forty-two, awaiting the go-ahead. Instead, Danny began his **dissertation** on education.

"I don't understand why we have to read all these stories. Hasn't the guy been dead for a couple hundred years? What has he got to tell us that we can learn from? I saw the story on an old TV program, and the guy's sick. Burying people in his basement and acting like nothing's wrong. I mean, what's it all about? What purpose is there for us to read about some other person's problem? What are they trying to do, make us all a bunch of crazies?" The questions were **valid**, worthy of a serious reply. I could imagine Mrs. Leopold answering it in her **picayune pedagogical dialectic** – "Because it's part of your course requirements" – as if that **substantiated** learning. If there was a reason for reading Poe, it surely had little to do with twentieth century **curricular dictates**. Without a **relevant** purpose – an individually applicable meaning – reading would indeed not be worth spending time on. All the **pedantically provincial** defenses could never **supplant** the one true reason for reading, and I didn't want to hide my firm supportiveness of the art from my closest friend.

"Danny, when you want to find out what's been happening, don't you sometimes read the newspaper?"

"Yeah, so?"

"And when you want to find out why your *RC-10* model needs to be cleaned, you check up on it in the latest car-model magazines, right?"

"Okay."

"And when we go to *Ala Moana Shopping Center* to check for the latest *Mach* boogie-board, you always seem to be up-to-date on the prices, the styles, the different things they have, right?"

"What's the point?" Danny asked impatiently.

"The point is, you're reading. You're reading to find out what's happening. You're reading to discover new information, to learn about everything there is to know so no one will rip you off or tell you how to think."

"So, I know that. What's the point?" Danny's curiosity was **piqued**.

"Poe wrote stories to tell you how some people think. He gave us a chance to step inside another person's shoes and feel how it is to be like that."

"Yeah, but I don't want to know what it's like to be crazy. There's enough of them around as it is."

"How do you know that, Danny?"

"Because that's the way they act, just like the person in the story."

My point was near completion. "And how did you find out that crazy people act and think like that?"

"Because I..." Danny stopped, avoiding the obvious reply. He didn't like to be led to the final answer, but he got the point nonetheless. "Okay, Jeremy, you've got a good way with words." He laughed good-naturedly, "You ought to be a teacher." I understood the **gist** of his argument – that teachers ought to teach in this way, showing practicality instead of necessity for reading. I had shown Danny why reading is worthwhile, and he reacted more positively to my **cogent rationale** than to what any of his teachers could ever hope to **inculcate** through their **stodgy, sanctimonious** instruction that did little more than **extirpate** student creativity and **stifle** meaningful discussion. Obviously, they weren't teaching; they were only telling.

"Ready, Danny?" I advanced.

"Shoot."

I **extracted** Mrs. Leopold's handout which served as a study guide for the upcoming exam on *The Tell-Tale Heart.* "Name three similes in the story." My eyes dropped. What did this question have to do with the story? With all the **verve** and **panache** of Poe's writing, how could the teacher ask such a **vapid, nugatory** question? My **premise** for the value of reading was dashed to pieces by Leopold's **obsolescent** study-guide. How many students in years-gone-by had learned that Poe is a great writer because he has similes in his stories? And how could a teacher, any teacher, seriously believe that a person who can't remember the specific similes used is therefore a poor reader of Poe? The entire educational system was becoming more backward as I looked more deeply and analyzed the assignments themselves. Working together with Danny, I now had the chance to review the questions rather than simply answer them to please the teacher. Now the questions needed to please me first, and I had little to say about what lay before my eyes.

Danny didn't know what a simile was. But he'd just told me more of the story and its **subtle implications** than most students could, including those who would probably get A's and B's on the exam. Danny had given the story personal **relevance** and had discovered what made the story worth reading or watching on television. I felt foolish asking such **otiose** questions **offensively unbecoming** of such an **acclaimed** and **profound** literary masterpiece. Perhaps Mr. Osmar had **encountered** the same **dilemma,** the same **paradox,** trying to create a learning environment amongst **insipidly weatherworn** study-guides and their **insipidly weatherworn** creators. No, I didn't think that becoming a teacher was something I would like.

"Danny, let's just try to do the best we can. That's all we can do, and I hope the teachers respect us for it."

"But they won't, you know that. They'll bounce me out so fast, they won't even remember my name next year."

I doubted whether anyone would soon forget his name, but I understood his point. He wasn't being recognized for his true self and instead was the **proverbial** 'bad egg' who would never change. **Ironically,** I **mused** over the likelihood that they would forget my name long before Danny's. In either case, it was obvious that most of the teachers couldn't care less for any of us, any of the nameless, faceless students whom they stepped over year after year – except for teachers like Mr. Osmar, who instead tried to relate to us and, as a result, faced the same fate at the feet of his fellow faculty members. It didn't pay to be a student or a good teacher.

Danny and I spent the next two hours **diligently** working on assorted homework assignments, many of which would be late and probably wouldn't receive credit anyway. But doing it all was better than nothing; at least there was a slim chance for survival.

By eight o'clock, we had wrapped up most of the exercises, Danny quietly watching as I explained and did most of the work. He was fascinated at my abilities, by my interest in the work and by my interest in helping him. I had never before worked so closely to assist in another's work; we had always played kids-games, from which we both benefitted. But little did he suspect that I probably gained more from helping him than he gained from my help. I absorbed everything with such **facility, retaining** all that I observed. In addition, I was helping my best friend in a man-sized crisis, sharing in a **euphoric camaraderie** words could not **aptly** describe. We were together as one, as one soul in two bodies. There was harmony and understanding. We had truly discovered the meaning of learning.

By eight o'clock, we had wrapped up most of the exercises, Danny quietly watching as I explained and did most of the work.

CHAPTER XV
Against The Odds

I waited anxiously for the next couple of days to pass in order to see what grades Danny had received on his homework and on his chapter exams. The homework exercises showed positive improvement, but Danny's **intuitive** analysis of the tests taken wasn't quite so favorable.

"I'll get the English exam back next week, but I really don't think I put it all together. Good try though, Jeremy."

My reassurance was always welcome. "Hang in there, Danny. We'll make it, together." And to reassure myself, I stopped by Mr. Osmar's office after school to **solicit** his assistance.

"Jeremy, I like your concern. Sure, I'll ask Mrs. Leopold and the others about Danny. It's the least I can do. But I can't promise anything. I'm not his teacher; they are."

Nothing more could be done. Danny and I had tried our best – we'd completed all the work assigned – and Mr. Osmar would now try to help tip the scales if he held any such power. I went home confident that Danny had **impressed** everyone satisfactorily to **warrant** their giving him another chance. After all, staying at Saint Paul meant so much for Danny, and surely no teacher would stand in the way of a serious attempt from one of their own students to stage a turnaround.

The results weren't **heartening**. Danny had **eked** out a C in his English exam, but Leopold gave him a zero for handing his homework in late. Mr. Salvo deducted one full grade on a lab report for what he **prejudicedly** labeled as "obviously not your own work," while Mrs. DiVicenzo gave him a C- for "excessively messy handwriting" on his topography quiz. All in all, Danny had managed to earn minimal marks for English, Physical Science and Geography; however, at this **piddling** pace the odds of raising the levels **sufficiently** before year-end were slim at best.

Danny had another plan, one I felt might eventually be suggested, one which I knew I would need to consider and analyze very carefully. "Jeremy," he began as we stood outside the classrooms during recess, "we need a special plan, anything it'll take to pass those semester exams. Something that's **foolproof**. It's the only chance I've got. And I need your help to make it work."

Danny **unveiled** his strategy, a scheme that reminded me of our prank to get my grades changed two years prior. This time, however, we would need to locate the exams before they were given. Danny felt we could have more success by finding out the problems – and answers – beforehand rather than trying to change the grades afterwards. Grade-changing in high school was not as easy a task as in junior high, but locating the semester exams would not be as difficult, because every high school teacher needed to have them prepared well in advance.

The idea would have sounded **practicable** if we were still kids, but I could no longer **condone** the act and the **opprobrious** nature of such **underhandedness**. The very idea of seeking an easy way out of learning **grated** against my better judgment. As children, we **relished** such **venturesome** challenges, caring little about the consequences; but as young responsible adults which we had supposedly become, such directions signified a **retrogression**, a **reversion** into irresponsible kids – the very thing we were trying to avoid being labeled as. I could not in good conscience applaud such an idea, yet I knew that any argument would surely **jeopardize** our friendship. I needed to decide, both for Danny's good and my own, whether to support the plan or turn **renegade**.

I chose a very indirect path of attack. "Danny, you remember when that guy Gary visited our school from *Alcoholics Anonymous*?"

"Yeah. What's that got to do with anything?"

"Hear me out, okay? This guy was really a pretty cool guy, but he was a lot more than just cool."

"Yeah, he was a drug user and a pusher. So what? Do you think I'm using drugs?" Danny was defensive.

"No, not at all. That's not my point. But listen, okay? He told us how he went through the skids, how he even stole from his dying grandfather because he needed the money to get a fix. And then he got busted finally and did almost six years at the State Pen. And even when he got out, he was right back on the streets again. He never changed."

"Yeah, but he did change," Danny added with less negativity. "He woke up one day and realized that he was on the bottom, and there was nothing left. He was...what did he say?"

"...'Spiritually, emotionally and psychologically bankrupt.' And he began to put his life back together, little by little, piece by piece. And you remember what he said about that experience?"

"Uh uh," Danny replied, interested in hearing the rest of the story.

"He said that you've got to hit the bottom to finally know what it means to make it in the world. He said he lived just to get high, but then he found that he was getting high just to live. For him, alcohol and drugs were his way of staying high, of avoiding the truth or facing the facts. Gary said he copped out to avoid feeling the pain, but he found out that he only made it worse for himself. And that's when he discovered that..."

" '...being cool is not so hot,'" Danny **interjected** excitedly. "Yeah, I remember that one really well. Yeah, it made sense," Danny nodded in agreement.

"And isn't that where we're at right now, with our backs against the wall at Saint Paul?" I included myself as a matter of courtesy, though I knew the problem affected only Danny. I tried to avoid losing my train of thought, uncertain how my analogy would tie together or how Danny would react to the story and its morality-theme. "We've got a chance to pick up the pieces and start fresh,"

I resumed, "but it's never gonna happen the way you've got it planned, Danny. That would be like Gary taking a drink or shooting up some heroin to make things get better. It wasn't the answer for Gary, it's not the answer for you. We can't beat the system by cheating ourselves. We'll never achieve true success or find spiritual happiness through self-deceit and **expedient** excuses; we've got to **confront** the problem head-on and grab the bull by the horns."

Danny caught my drift – I was refusing to help him in his plan. But rather than launch a **volley** of **unexpurgated expletives** at me and storm out, he continued our discussion in truest adult maturity. "Okay, so you're saying we need to do it by studying. That's fine, if it works. But what if it doesn't work? We're putting a lot on the line in the name of honesty."

"That's right, Danny," I **affirmed**, "I know we are. But if you come out ahead, you can say that you did it despite the system's screwups."

"And what if I don't make it?"

"Then you still come out ahead, even if the system refuses to accept it. Either way, you win."

Danny was too practical to submit **obsequiously** to such **academic dialectics**, yet neither did he pursue the debate. He recognized what lay at stake and instead **opted** to **capitulate** in behalf of our friendship. "Okay, Jeremy, we'll try it. Like you say, we'll win either way, I guess. I sure hope you're right, though." He leaned back, biting his lip in **contemplation**.

In the background, coming from the music speakers of the lunchroom, the lyrics from *Lean On Me* **wafted** through the air, **subliminally emboldening** my **resolve**:

> *"Lean on me when you're not strong,*
> *I'll give you strength, I'll keep you holding on."*

The **oracular** words were truly meant for Danny and me.

"We can't beat the system by cheating ourselves."

CHAPTER XVI
The Ceremony

Our Sophomore year edged closer to completion as students impatiently anticipated the final, **climactic** events on the school calendar. The Sophomore/Junior prom was scheduled for May 16th, one week after finals, with class-ring ceremonies taking place May 1st. I elected to ask Linda Kilbraith to the prom, almost in **memorialized exultation** of the triumph Danny and I enjoyed when we successfully pulled the wool over her eyes. I owed her something in return for what she had **unwittingly** done for us, and since neither she nor I were **eminent socialites** in the campus **clique**, we almost seemed the perfect match: a school-teacher's daughter and a former Striped Panther.

Danny asked Sarah if she wanted to go, but he chose a most unusual moment to do so. Although most Sophomore boys carefully planned the time and place to ask their girlfriends – or hopeful girlfriends-to-be – if they wished to share the special evening together, Danny asked Sarah during lunch, as I looked on. It was as though he were afraid to talk secretly with her, as though he feared rejection should the question be asked in private.

She politely agreed, though more out of **deference** than true desire. The mood just didn't seem right, as though a slight **rift** had emerged between the two. I waited until after school to **substantiate** my suspicions.

"Are you two fighting, Danny?" I inquired as we walked together to the bus stop after school.

"What makes you ask such a stupid question? Of course not." Danny was hiding something. His voice was shaky and uncertain, **subtly beseeching** me to persist in my **prodding** to **unearth** the real truth.

"Okay, *Romeo*," I began in light-hearted appeal, "you're not planning to **elope** with her and leave me out in the cold, now are you?" The moment of **jollity** melted the ice and **stimulated** further discussion.

"Jeremy, promise not to tell anyone what I'm gonna tell you?"

"Promise," I **asserted solemnly**, readying myself for the **momentous** confessional **revelation**.

"You remember when Sarah and I were talking the other day during lunch? That was when you thought we were talking about my grades."

"Yeah, sure, I remember it well." I'd never forget the final words he'd said to me: 'Nobody'll ever replace you on that, guaranteed.'

"Well, we were talking about getting more serious, like going steady, and all that."

"So what did she say?" I could sense that my suspicions were not **baseless**: Things weren't perfect between the two **star-crossed** lovers.

"She really didn't say anything. All she said was that she had to think about it awhile longer, 'til she was sure."

"Is that all?" I added with a **palpable** sigh of relief. "I thought she was dumping you or something." I didn't mean to be so **blunt**, but the relief of the moment unlocked my worst fears. Danny was in the same position as every other Sophomore in every high school in the good-old United States of America, trying to lay hands on the pride of every young teenager's affection: one girl to call his very own. And just like every other teenage boy everywhere, Danny had discovered that the road to victory was neither easy nor a straight line.

"Heck, you've got nothing to worry about," I continued. "Give her time to think on it and you'll bag her like a sack of potatoes." This wasn't my ideal image of what having a girlfriend was like, but for the sake of simplicity and **callow frivolity**, I **interjected** the **crass** and **hackneyed** analogy.

"Yeah, I guess you're right, Jeremy. In fact, you always seem to be right. You amaze me sometimes. You ought to be a teacher."

I was beginning to get annoyed at the repetitious remark regarding my professional **attributes**. Wouldn't it have just been easier for Danny to say "a successful lawyer." At least there would be more money and perhaps even fewer disappointments in that role.

Danny continued **elaborating** upon his fears, however. "That's why I asked Sarah while you were there. I didn't think she'd say 'No' while you were around. I know she likes you a lot."

I **tempered** any suspicions that might otherwise have **festered** deep in Danny's heart. "I'm going with Linda Kilbraith, so don't go jumping to conclusions quite so fast."

"That's not what I meant, you know that. It's just that she seems to be acting really cool to me, like there's something else on her mind, but she won't tell me. No, I don't think it's someone else." His thoughts suddenly gathered what I had said to him. "Linda Kilbraith, that old bag? You're going to the prom with her? Why? Have you no decency and self-respect? My oh my, I've been neglecting my best friend, and now he's mating with the devil's daughter. Oh, we are in a bad situation, aren't we, son?" The **somber** atmosphere was instantly **vivified** with the **whimsically jocose raillery**. Danny's **predicament** didn't really seem so **dire** after all, and with the tension now **defused** a renewed confidence emerged. We felt certain that everything would **resolve** itself without further confusion.

☆ ☆

The May 1st ring-ceremonies event quickly arrived, and all the Sophomore and Junior boys **converged** after school at Campbell Auditorium to pay for the rings and prepare for the annual **ritual** in which each boy would present his **lady fair** with the token of his **esteem**. This presentation was **tantamount** to a formal invitation to the Junior prom. Although called 'Junior,' the event was open to all high school students, with Sophomores and Juniors equally in attendance. The Seniors awaited their 'private' prom and therefore shied away from the secondary engagement. The Junior prom marked, for Sophomores and a few Freshmen, their first **entree** socially into the adult world, and the boys were understandably nervous and excited. Meanwhile, the girls – the recipients of the rings – would be arriving an hour later, when the ceremony officially **commenced**. The proceedings would last but fifteen or twenty minutes, yet the thrills of establishing a social relationship following the traditional guidelines were a lifelong anticipation for a great many of the boys.

Danny and I each paid our $45 and received in exchange the **chartreuse** boxes containing the class rings, each **elaborately** adorned with a green-and-white border surrounding an **embossed** sculpture of a ferocious tiger. The receipt for the paid rings **commemorated** for many the first such document **validating** and **authenticating** their devotion to another, but for Danny and for me the purchase represented nothing more than an unwanted additional donation out of our own pockets. Danny had spoken of the ceremony as "forced marriage," to which I had little to add, not seriously or even humorously entertaining marriage to Linda Kilbraith.

During the **respite** between ring pick-up and arrival of the girls, I sneaked off to Miller's Annex, two short buildings to the east. The walk took less than a minute and **afforded** me the chance to see what I had missed at the monthly Panther meetings.

The door of the Annex was unlocked, so I entered and viewed the room whose walls were decorated with graffiti and knife carvings. "SP rules" was the most **prevalent** wording, but the totality of the writings could barely entertain a two-year-old. There was nothing of value in the room; I realized how little I had missed at the meetings.

I hurried back to the auditorium just in time to see Sarah walk in with Linda Kilbraith. Apparently the two had been talking and knew who their respective **beaus** were to be.

Once gathered, the entire student body was **segregated** into boys and girls while the chaperoning teachers stood in the front of the auditorium, behind wooden podiums. The ceremony was begun without further **ado**, teachers and students alike anxious to conclude the event and return to normal activities.

Mr. Farheim, friend to none, opened the ceremony speaking on behalf of the teachers of Saint Paul. "Okay, settle down. I said shut up! You people get worse every year. Let's get some quiet here so we can get through. I'm sure you've all got exams to study for, so let's just finish this up as quickly as we can."

Danny and I...received the class rings, each elaborately adorned with...an embossed sculpture of a ferocious tiger.

The old man had soured the event for many who had waited months for the precious moments. Farheim had reminded them that exams were right around the corner, that this assembly was but a necessary irritant which he and the other teachers were **obliged** to **preside** over, and that once past, the event would soon be forgotten and of no further significance.

Twenty-five minutes later, the **fiasco** was over. Linda and I parted company amicably, bidding our fondest farewells until we would meet again in class or at the prom, whichever came first. Danny and Sarah were locked up in a more serious conversation. I stood **idly** by while the music **blared** in the background:

> *"Sometimes when we touch, the honesty's too much*
> *And I have to close my eyes and hide;*
> *I want to hold you 'til I die, 'til we both break down and cry;*
> *I want to hold you 'til the fear in me subsides."*

Had the teachers listened to the words, they'd never have allowed the song to be played. They would have found it **obscene**, the same way they seemed to view everything involving youth, innocence and **heartfelt** emotions.

After five minutes on the sidelines, I wandered closer to the two. They were in the heat of conversation. The mood appeared somewhat tense. "Hi Sarah," I **interposed** in a tone of sociable friendliness. "How's it going, Danny?"

Sarah had apparently concluded her thoughts and was simply listening to Danny when I interrupted. My words provided her with the perfect **cue** to bid **adieu**. "Oh hi, Jeremy. My, we've been talking so long and I need to study for those semester exams. Anyway, I'll meet you at 7 p.m. at *Oka's Market* on the 16th, okay Danny?" And with those words, Sarah smiled politely and glided gracefully out the auditorium doors as though an angel **summoned** back to the **celestial firmament**.

The conversation ended peaceably enough, so I ventured to **ascertain** the **gist** of the discussion. "What'd she say, Danny?"

"Oh, not much."

"You guys were talking for ten minutes. It didn't sound like 'not much' to me."

Danny shrugged his shoulders, looking down at his black leather *Florsheims* which matched **flawlessly** with his white *Jimmy 'Z* and his dark blue velour pullover. "She's really hard to predict. I can't tell what's bothering her. There's something on her mind, but I can't figure it out."

"Maybe exams, Danny?" I suggested.

"Could be. I guess that's it." But I could sense that he wasn't convinced. Perhaps he'd find out at the prom. "Well," he concluded as he looked up, "I guess it's over. We spent $45 each and now we've got nothing to show for it."

"We've got memories, Danny."

"Yeah, sure. I'll always remember fat-face Farheim talking to us like we were a bunch of dogs. Well, let's go, Mr. J. It's getting stuffy in here."

CHAPTER XVII
Coming Clean

I didn't hear much about Sarah the following week. Danny and I were busily in the midst of year-end exams, finishing the semester exams before being subjected to those **interminable** finals. Danny's homework grades were **impressive**, due in great part to my guidance, but I wasn't certain whether he would **retain** the information necessary to pass the **crucial** examinations. The finals were of special concern since they tended to reflect material covered during the past year, half of which Danny had all but missed.

We worked together after school and after my newspaper route, cramming as much possible before Danny's attention **waned** and studying had reached its daily limit. I managed to also keep up with my own studies, though most of the classes and content were vastly different. Fortunately, I had taken most of Danny's classes before and had **sufficient** notes to assist us wherever explanations were needed. I couldn't help Danny memorize the material, nor could I be sure he understood the concepts, but I offered my best guidance and hoped he would apply what was covered when it was his turn to take the exams.

After each daily study session, we would walk to Waikiki and reflect upon the day's events, eventually reaching farther back and reflecting upon our past years at Saint Paul. One afternoon, our topic of discussion drifted to our present accomplishments and future **aspirations**. The ideas between us flowed smoothly, just as they did when we were kids but in a more mature level of conversation. We had each learned to analyze, to question, to evaluate situations as they affected us. One could scarcely imagine that Danny – the **maverick nonconformist** and rebel – and I – a conservative-looking honor student – thought the same way, could share our thoughts in a one-to-one **mutual** understanding, and could each display signs of having been **amply** educated for our age. Danny, in fact, tended to have a better common-sense approach to matters than I, placing him at an even higher level of **intuitive** intelligence than I myself possessed. The teachers' **outmoded** evaluations didn't serve justice for Danny, nor probably for a hundred other students mislabeled as 'slow,' '**dyslexic**,' or simply 'unmotivated.'

"Danny," I began without **reserve** as we were walking out of his house, "what do you want to do when you grow up?"

Danny smiled in amusement by my phrase 'when you grow up.' "I thought we are already grown up. Isn't that what you've been telling me for months?"

"Well, you know what I mean. What's in your plans?"

"Well let's see, Mr. J. First I'll be on the honor roll and then graduate as class **valedictorian**, and then–"

"Seriously, Danny," I interrupted. "Are you planning to join the Army or something? They could use a few good men like you."

"That's the Marines, you schnook," he added **sportively**, setting me straight. "Naw, they need good men, not smart ones like you and me."

"How about getting married or going to college?" I was curious whether one of these **evocative** questions might **kindle** his imagination.

"College, maybe. Who knows. It's so far away from today, all I want to do now is keep my head above water."

"How about the Panthers? Do you still need them?"

"I've been thinking about that, too. Chip seems to have more things to say every time we have a meeting, and **frankly** I don't think we really did very much this past year. I just think everybody got tired of flattening the teachers' tires. That was Sanders' 'bag' but not mine."

I had **surmised** that the Panthers had gone through a lengthy period of inactivity. But it wasn't because 'everybody' got tired of the mischievous pranks – only Danny. The soldiers still followed whatever their leader suggested, but as Danny matured his misdirected enthusiasm **ebbed**. He was no longer one of the team, and his followers in turn found more **commonality** with Chip, who fit perfectly into the role as president of a group of **malcontents** and trouble-makers.

"So what's left then, huh Danny? You think maybe we can try something new when we're Juniors." I was casting ideas out though in the **nascent** stages of a brainstorming session, uncertain how anything would be interpreted.

"I think I'll just wait and find out. It's hard to plan when so many people hate you. I don't think there's a teacher on campus who wants me around after the past couple of years, and I guess they still know I'm president of the Panthers. Nothing's changed."

"Danny, you've changed in some ways. You've changed a whole lot. But you haven't changed your true self. You've always stuck to your ideals, your inner sense of justice. And you've never changed in being a friend to me." My voice cracked on the word 'friend,' my eyes clouding up, the words coming in spurts. "And you'll always...be my friend. God knows how much I like you, man..." The words had rushed out before I could **censor** them, and my eyes reacted with a gush of tears at the **lachrymose** confession.

"Jeremy, stop that. Gosh, everybody's looking." But his eyes were also watery, and I could see that we were helplessly caught in our own **maudlin** moment. We ducked out from the street and sat on a retaining wall, waiting for the next words. They came from Danny's lips.

"Jeremy, stop that. Gosh, everybody's looking."

"Why did you help me, Jeremy? Why didn't you just let me fight by myself and learn the hard way?"

I couldn't establish the specific tone of the question. "Are you angry that I helped you, Danny?"

"No, man, but nobody's ever helped me before. My mom's never done half the things you've done for me. I don't know anybody who ever cared a crap about me, except Sarah and you." He then corrected himself in a way that left me **thunderstruck**. "No, I mean only you."

"Why not Sarah? She's been a true friend to both of us." I stared confusedly into his eyes.

"I know that, but that's different. She's a great girl, the best friend you could ask for in a girl, but I mean, well, you've done things for me – not just listen to me – and you've given me advice. You really have helped, something I've never done for anyone else in my life, ever. Damn, and now listen to what I'm saying. You've got me crying and I don't know why. I've never cried in my life before. My mom could beat the daylights of me and I wouldn't cry."

My eyes drifted down to the grass below us. I knew he had run out of words for the moment. "Look, Danny, crying is for hurt and crying is for joy. This one's for joy, so don't feel that it's a bummer. When's the last time you felt good? And I don't mean watching someone else get screwed up and then laughing at him."

Danny **pondered** awhile, also looking toward the grass as though we both belonged in the world of ants and aphids, hiding amongst the blades of green that towered above the soil. "I don't know. I don't really know what it is that'll make me happy. Man, you gotta have a reason to be happy."

"You've got a reason, Danny. It's the same reason that you can cry. It's knowing that everything's not so bad, that you can enjoy life without thinking you're weird. That you can let loose and feel free. It doesn't matter who you are or where you are. It feels so damned good to get those feelings out." I began to gain strength from my **sobering** comments, looking up from the grass which suddenly seemed an inappropriate place to hide in.

Danny looked up at me. "Okay, Jeremy, what if you're right. Where does it get me? I'm gonna laugh and cry myself right out of Saint Paul. What do I do, laugh at the teachers? Cry at them? Tell me."

I became instantly and shockingly aware that Danny was reaching an emotional crisis, a change I hadn't detected until this very moment. All his **façades** which had been masking the true inner person were gone, and Danny, stripped of all **pretension** and deception, gazed into my eyes for guidance, for a **compassionate** answer that could only be shared between two friends as close as Danny and me.

My heart began to pump faster. I felt squeezed between two immovable objects: the school system and our own needs. Doubtless, the rigid structure of education wouldn't **yield** an inch to our pleas, and yet we couldn't simply abandon our own goals and **succumb** to it. I had no answer. We ended the conversation **unresolved**. Little did I know at the time that Danny would not leave the question **unresolved**. He would find an answer. He did find an answer.

CHAPTER XVIII
Complications

Danny and I worked closely throughout the remainder of the week, but I knew he was thinking deeply about what we had said, grateful for my support and hopeful that our friendship could weather the **turbulent** storm. However, the focus of the proceedings was abruptly **diverted** from school-grades the following week when Sarah intercepted Danny and me walking to school.

"Here's your ring, Danny. Sorry." The words came out **curtly**, after which Sarah turned and walked away in hasty gliding steps. We both stopped still in our tracks, Danny staring at the ring that lay abandoned in his right hand while I watched Sarah depart. I could tell she was crying.

Danny was **stunned**. "This isn't real. Tell me it isn't real, Jeremy." He stood motionless, his eyes fixed on the ring, the only thing remaining from what appeared to be a **blatant** confirmation of love **unrequited**. "Say something to me, Jeremy. Please."

I didn't know where to begin. The action went far beyond anything I could have ever imagined possible. But I needed to respond, to say something to keep Danny's mind from wandering in thought too far.

"I guess she'll tell us later. I don't think she meant for it to hurt, Danny. I think something happened to her. Maybe some problem in her family."

"You think that's it," Danny uttered mechanically, looking up at me. "Do you think it was because of that? You don't think it was because of me?"

I **contemplated leavening** the atmosphere with a humorous **quip**, but this was neither the time nor the place. "No, not because of you. Something's happened and she's the one who's suffering. You better go after her and find out what. I think she needs you."

Danny hesitated. "I think I'll give her some time to herself. I'll see her at lunch. If you see her, Jeremy, please tell her to wait for me."

"You can count on me, Danny."

"Thanks, Jeremy. I know I can always count on you."

Danny departed for his first class, slipping the ring into his shirt pocket. I remained behind, hiding my tears but **venting** my frustration. "God, why does everything seem to be happening all at once?" The words echoed quietly but left no **consolation**. The tears began to fall.

☆ ☆

"Here's your ring, Danny. Sorry."

I did not see Sarah before lunch, but I discovered the secret from Linda. Sarah's parents had sold their house and were moving to Georgia, where her father had been offered an executive position with a local radio station. Sarah had known for a couple of months about the plan to move, but until yesterday the house had not been sold. Now, everything was definite and the family would be moving the day after school ended. Sarah would be in Georgia on the day the prom would be held.

Linda offered me some words of advice for Danny, meant in all sincerity. "Stand by him, Jeremy. The news is going to hurt him, I know. He's a very sensitive boy. Watch out for him, he needs you now more than ever."

Linda had apparently a much deeper understanding of and appreciation for Danny, recognizing the pain he was suffering and **discerning** the lost child hiding beneath the layers of **ostentation** and **bombast**. I began to wonder whether the story that Danny told me about changing my grades was totally accurate. Maybe there was more to the story than I had been told. Maybe much more.

I sought Danny between classes, but he was nowhere to be found. Finally at lunch, I saw him. Linda had approached him after class and had led him to the cafeteria. The two were talking when I arrived.

Linda motioned for me to sit down, as Danny continued speaking with her. He had obviously learned what had happened and was **resigning** himself to accept the **incontrovertible** and **irrevocable** truth.

Danny was now alone. He had lost his date, his friend, his **confidante**. The system had denied him the opportunity of even attending the prom. He was skidding near the bottom, and yet the floor seemed to drop lower with each successive stroke of **ill** fate.

I remembered Linda's advice and offered a **viable** option to address the sadness. "Danny, let's go out tonight and hit the town, like we used to."

The suggestion fell flat. Danny was in no mood to **entertain** thoughts of pleasure or escape. "No, I think I'm gonna sit on this for a while," he replied unemotionally. "I don't want to try to forget it. It won't do me any good. You told me so yourself. You can't run away from the truth."

"But what can you do about it? My advice is to forget about it and ask someone else to go to the prom."

Danny turned his whole body toward me while sitting on the cafeteria bench. "Do you know what you're asking me to do? It's like telling me that friends aren't important, that it's okay to just drop one and find a replacement. Is that what you're saying?" Danny was **confronting** me with the **quandary** that had undoubtedly faced millions of people in all of history: the question "How do you say goodbye?".

"I don't know what I'm saying exactly, Danny, but I know that you can't stop this from happening, so you've got to learn to live with it."

"Like my mother has learned to live with my father. Like we've got to live with the teachers. Like our whole screwed-up life is just one big game of listening and obeying. No way, man, I'm not gonna take that for an answer. I've got my own self to answer to, and I'm not going to let any lousy news change me from doing what I want. The whole world can go to hell." He jumped up explosively, banging the table with his fist, and stormed out the building, attracting attention from others who felt he was acting tough again, a reflection of just how little people really knew about him.

Linda repeated her words of caution to me, adding, "Remember, he's a very sensitive boy. I knew what he did for you. My mom would never understand, but that's what happens when you forget what being young is all about. Watch after him, Jeremy. You're all he's got left."

"Watch after him, Jeremy. You're all he's got left."

CHAPTER XIX
A Neighboring Dispute

Sarah kept to herself for the remainder of the semester, speaking little to anyone and avoiding Danny and me as much as possible. I did manage to share my thoughts with her for a few minutes here and there, but she seemed already **resigned** to her parents' wishes, certain that she would never be returning to the islands. I asked if it would be too difficult to keep a romance alive by mail, but she shied away from the suggestion. It was the end of her affairs with the people at Saint Paul, and as though an angel of innocence she chose to look toward brighter horizons in a new land. I could not affect her reasoning, so I turned my interest instead to Danny, who was accepting the same fate but in a less **optimistic** manner.

Danny seemed **irreparably distracted** by the incident, which limited his concentration and his interest to study. I tried to change his attitude, but his thoughts were on more personally **relevant** matters.

"What can *you* do about it, Danny?" I asked **sternly**. "Nothing now, so don't screw up where it really counts, on those exams."

"What's so important about exams? They don't accomplish anything. They won't change anything."

"But they'll keep you at Saint Paul. Isn't that what you want, to stay at Saint Paul?"

"I don't know anymore. I don't really care, either. How about we skip studying tonight? I'm not really in the mood." Danny appeared **despondent**.

"Then we go out. It doesn't matter where, but anywhere."

My **emphatic** response **enlivened** him a bit. "Thanks for the thought, Jeremy," he answered, "but you've got to study. I want to be alone, anyway." He then concluded the conversation abruptly and strode swiftly away, adding, "I'll call you tonight."

But Danny didn't call, and I didn't see him in school for the rest of the week.

☆ ☆

The following Monday began finals-week, and as I waited for the bus I hoped and prayed that Danny was already on it. It arrived shortly, I entered and immediately **espied** Danny sitting **sullenly** in one of the front seats. I welcomed him with **unbridled** enthusiasm. "Boy was I worried about you, Danny. Thank God you're okay."

"Thanks, Jeremy," he replied **stoically**.

I pursued the mystery. "Where were you last week? I didn't see you at all."

"Oh, I guess I had to sort things out for myself. I even got a little studying in edgewise." He seemed very **robotic** in his tone of voice, as though he were on medication.

"Well, I'm glad you're back." I rested comfortably next to him, satisfied that he would at least give his best effort during the critical week of finals. I then focused on my own studies as the bus took us closer to our destination, though deep in the **recesses** of my consciousness the image of Danny **hovered** above each theorem and formula.

The first two classes went smoothly for me, as I breezed through my Algebra II exam and prepared myself mentally for the upcoming two-hour biology exam, which would extend through periods three and four. The final exam week actually lasted only three days, each class spanning two periods during this special **modified** scheduling.

The fireworks began during fourth period across the hall in Mr. Salvo's physical science room. In the middle of my biology final, I could hear some **intermittent** clatter, as though someone were throwing books across the room. It disturbed my concentration just as I was about to write down the formula for the process of photosynthesis. Looking up from my exam, I noticed that the entire class was fully **cognizant** of the **raucous** noise. Nobody was working on the exam. We all listened **attentively** to detect whether there was a fight between students erupting in Salvo's room.

The class across the hall suddenly exploded with a **dissonant** clash between what appeared to be the teacher and a student.

"Don't tell me what I see, young man," the instructor **retorted imperiously**.

"And don't tell me how to act. You're not my mother," the student countered angrily.

"I told you I'll tear up anyone's exam if they cheat, so don't give me your cock-and-bull excuses." The prize at stake was obviously the final-exam grade.

Someone in my class commented softly "Wow, that guy's in hot water. Bad timing, I tell you."

I knew who the student was. It was bad timing, indeed.

Danny persisted in his **defiance**. "You think that a guy's gotta cheat just to pass your test? Then maybe you better rewrite your tests so people can't cheat. And don't accuse me of something you can't prove."

"Oh, I can prove it all right," and then we could barely hear what appeared to be the sound of something being ripped several times. Someone's exam was now in pieces.

The class across the hall suddenly exploded with a dissonant clash between . . . the teacher and a student. I knew who the student was. It was bad timing, indeed.

But Danny returned the blow without pause. "You think you have all the answers, but you know nothing about us. And you know even less about teaching. You're the failure, not me. Your shriveled-up excuse of a test proves how little you're worth. You haven't had a human thought for years, and you wouldn't recognize one if it bit you on the ass. You can take your miserable test and your **festered** life straight to hell. The world will be a better place without you." Danny had buried the hatchet deep into the system, etching his opinion loudly for all to hear.

Then all was silent for a moment, followed by footsteps stomping out of the physical science room. Nobody had objected to the exit; there were no other sounds to be heard.

Without surprise, I didn't see Danny after school. He had obviously gone home early, bypassing his geography exam as a result. There was little doubt that he had sealed his fate and that all the help in the world could not reverse the damage done today.

Mr. Salvo had always accused Danny of cheating, either on homework or on tests, ever since I began to help him. Salvo's **entrenched** opinions were **unappeasable** and **unalterable**: A poor student would always be a poor student. He could have given 90% of his grades out after the first week of school; he had each student conveniently **stereotyped** by that time. And to him, Danny was "trouble," nothing but a threat to him and his class. Every question Danny had raised early in the year was met with the same answer: "If you'd been listening, you'd know what I said." Danny stopped asking questions and started his rapid decline in the class, eventually not handing in any of the work until I began to assist in its production. Salvo had taught Danny that it didn't pay to study or to ask questions and, once convinced, Danny **impressed** upon Salvo that he was indeed going to be a non-productive student. Salvo had created this situation, and now he condemned Danny for the very attitude he had **engendered**.

Whether Danny really cheated on the final was of no consequence. Salvo had his list of 'bad' students and was eager to find an excuse to exaggerate each student's behavior to help support his **distorted** perspective. However, Danny hadn't **succumbed** to Salvo's **overbearing countenance**; he didn't afford Salvo the satisfaction of stamping the final words to the **reprimand**. Salvo had attempted to humiliate Danny in front of his **peers** as well as to the careful ear of all surrounding classes, but Danny had issued the tongue-lashing **finale** and didn't give Salvo a chance to defend himself. Danny had emerged the **victor**. He had not compromised his own beliefs. He had not sold out to the system.

But he was indeed in **dire straits** at Saint Paul. All that was left was to await the official word from the principal's office. I wanted to be with him when the phone call came, so I rushed after school to Danny's house. If he would be made a **martyr** by his mom, at least I would be there to defend him. I was not afraid of his mom. Friendship overpowered fear.

Danny was in his room when I arrived at his house. The **debacle** at school had left him **discomfited**, and he welcomed my appearance.

"So you heard about it, huh, Jeremy?"

"I was right there, across the hall, in Room 53. You really stuck up for your own beliefs, didn't you, **Hercules**?" I tried to lighten up the atmosphere with the half-humorous reference.

"Yeah, I guess I'm king of the mountain, the mighty Panther." he answered with **morose resignation**.

"No, you are who you are, who you have chosen to be," I stressed **assertively**. "You're not anybody else; you've never tried to be someone else. I don't think you ever needed to hit the bottom. I think you've learned a lot and I don't think it came from hitting the bottom. That was Gary's trip, but he was and always will be an alcoholic, a drug-user. He said it himself, he is always going to be the most likely person to start doing it again. A person really never changes; he simply realizes who he is and then **safeguards** himself so he doesn't get into hot water that he can't handle. But you did handle the situation; you're no pushover. No, you don't have to change who you are. You're everything we all want to be. You're the only one who hasn't let the system change you at all. It might not change anyone in the long run, but it'll sure take a while for us to get back to who we really are. But you, you haven't changed at all. Danny, you've put up with so much bullshit from so many people, and you're still the same person I've known for years."

"No, I've changed a bit," Danny echoed softly. "I'm not the kid I was when we ripped off the stores for kicks. That doesn't mean anything to me anymore. There's no reason to do it, and I guess you showed me that this year. You showed me that we've got to each stand up for our own beliefs and follow our own dreams, even if they aren't what the teachers want."

"Screw the teachers," I screamed. I had gained enough disgust of teachers today not to want the word spoken.

"No, don't say that," Danny replied sympathetically. "Don't feel that just because we've got a rotten system, that all teachers are bad. It's not true. You've been the best teacher I've ever had. I really mean that, Jeremy."

With such **heartfelt** words spoken, our eyes **commenced** to cloud **synchronously**. We were so closely **enmeshed** in spirit that we could sense one another's emotional changes, an **affective epiphany** that **dilated** our sensibilities and **infused** our consciousness with an almost **epileptic vibrancy**. The power **defied** explanation. We were two **diaphanous** clouds floating **ethereally** side by side in **kaleidoscopic kinship**, drifting together **sans** the **corporeal complexities** and **mundane** annoyances that **plagued** the world below. We had become two **cosmic** bodies with **singular** identity interested only in **intimately savoring** one another's friendship and in reflecting on the best of times.

Resting on the floor and propping our heads up against Danny's bed, we gazed out the bedroom window to the street below and the ocean that lay beyond. The moment had come for dreaming, for

purging our souls and recognizing who we really were, **irrespective** of what the teachers tried to tell us.

"Danny, remember the day you took revenge against the *Exotic Gifts* shop in Waikiki?"

"Yeah, as clearly as if it happened yesterday. Why?"

"I was wondering how it felt to pull off that **caper**?"

"You did the work, I simply put the idea together."

"Yeah, but you were the one who got to read about it in the newspaper. How did it feel?"

"I don't know. I guess I felt **avenged**. Maybe I should have felt a bit **remorseful**, but I never really did. Why are you asking me this now?"

"I'm not sure. You know, somehow I always had the feeling that there was something bad about doing it. All the while, I didn't consider the **rationale** behind the action. We're brought up with morality and **righteousness**, and the two don't mix at all. If Jesus were alive today, he'd be thrown in jail for the things he **defiantly** did; it's as though everybody's supposed to be a follower now, as if nobody has the right to speak up for themselves. I never thought I'd say this, but you know, you were right in what you did. I don't know if they were the best-laid plans, but nobody has the right to put you down for taking a stand and acting on it. That's between a person and his conscience, nobody else." I **pondered** what I had just said, shocked by my support of such **unbecoming** behavior and yet thrilled by my **convictions**. I knew it made sense, **unorthodox** though it might have appeared to me before.

Danny reacted with surprise. "I think you're right, Jeremy. I think a person's got to speak up for what he believes, even if it kills him. Sometimes the truth is too powerful to hide. It's like something deep inside that's gotta come out. I guess Salvo unlocked the door for me, and I let loose with my sermon."

We laughed together, grateful for this moment of **divine** interpersonal **discourse** to reflect on and share our feelings. We had discovered an **unalterable** truth behind the lesson. We understood that no teacher, no school, no system can change what is real. They can attempt to **obfuscate** the truth, make **superficial alterations**, insert **factious innuendos** and **distort** them, but they can never erase or change what is and will always be the truth when the **façade** is exposed. Danny had blown the cover away, and the classes in the vicinity were all **privy** to the real reason for Salvo's actions: He was seeking to alter student behaviors in a **premeditated, self-aggrandizing** manner to uphold his **pretentious, pompous ideology** that the **academic elite** are **inherently** superior to the **minions** they **condescendingly** refer to as students. He'd been doing so for years, but now the **perfidious** plot had been laid bare, and the **perpetrator** lay stripped to the bone, naked for all to see in his true form. He was a **charlatan**, a shallow man whose very existence was **predicated** on deceit. He was

The moment had come for dreaming, for purging our souls and recognizing who we really were...

a **despicable** excuse of a teacher, even as a human being. Danny had sacrificed himself to let the truth be known. *Judas Iscariot* had been exposed, and student **self-esteem** was restored, even if only temporarily.

☆ ☆

Later that afternoon, while we were still **opining** the merits of life, Danny's mom knocked **indelicately** on the bedroom door. "Danny, come out here right away." The school had evidently just called.

Danny and I got up and headed towards the **inferno**. "Well, here we go again," he said, prepared to be subjected once more to his mom's **unrelenting tirade**. He wouldn't defend his individual rights against her. He had no rights in her house.

The first thing Mrs. Oakley did was dismiss me from her presence, leaving me no alternative but to obey her **peremptory directive**. The **immediacy** of her command left no room for debate, not even a chance to for me sneak in a word in Danny's behalf. The front door was open before she finished her first sentence.

"You better leave, Jeremy," Danny whispered. "I'll call you later."

"Okay, but if you don't call me, I'll contact you."

"Thanks, Jeremy," Danny added, aware he would probably be grounded and restricted from making phone calls for a long while. I only hoped his mom would at least let him receive calls.

As I returned home on the bus, I sought in some **vicarious** way to transport and **materialize** myself to the very **corporeal** being of my **kindred spirit**, absorbing the punishment as I **transubstantiated** in his **stead**. But **alas**, my **frail mortal** condition could **avail** me no further than allow me to dwell on my soulmate's misfortune and **ruminate** whether he had already been suspended from St. Paul. Much would be revealed when I next got in touch with Danny, but even if I wasn't able to reach him I knew I'd have my answer the following day. If Danny was in school, then the news would not have been so serious.

I did not see Danny for the rest of the week, nor was I able to reach him on the telephone. His mom answered once, **tersely** replying "Danny's not home. Don't call him again." The news was bad.

CHAPTER XX
Evaluating The System

As year-end school festivities rapidly approached, everyone rushed to meet schedules and deadlines. Preparations were completed for the Senior-class graduation and the Junior and Senior proms. In addition, the Striped Panthers held a special meeting at Chip's request to elect a new president for the coming year, now that it was learned Danny would not be returning. The meeting was brief, without **pomp and circumstance**. Danny's name was barely mentioned, reflecting the **capricious** nature of the allegiance the Panthers held for one another, time measured in **fugitive**, **ephemeral** moments. Chip painted for me the scene in the simplicity in which the meeting was apparently conducted: "We voted for a new president. I won."

"Did you say anything about Danny?" I questioned.

"Why should we? He's history."

And that was it. Danny was 'history,' ancient and forgotten like the nameless **predecessors** who had ruled the Panthers' lair. Chip would one day also become merely another faceless name carved into the walls of Miller's Annex, a fate he richly deserved.

I concentrated, meanwhile, on my own **academic** needs, securing another notch for myself on the honor roll. The exams seemed **trite** and meaningless, **comprised** of a **mélange** of **marginal** questions and a **paucity** of **provocative** ones, reflective of a curriculum **reliant** on education by **rote** – questions as **vacuous** as "List five organelles and their functions in the cell"; "Define what is meant by 'creative imagery'"; "Trace the downfall of Napoleon Bonaparte." Lacking intellectual stimulation, the exams exposed the **folly** and **banality** of **academically picayune pedagogy**.

No matter what class the exam was for, the questions all sounded the same: impersonal, irrelevant to the student, and simply products of a bored teacher with no commitment to make education challenging for the students. It wasn't education at all; it was a puppet-factory, and only Danny had cut his strings and declared his freedom.

After the final day of exams passed, I met with Linda, firming our plans for the prom. She wasn't an unlikable person after all; in fact, we seemed to share similar outlooks, theories and perspectives. We each questioned why things are done in such **haphazard** fashion, such as **evidenced** in school. And like me, she had few friends because she didn't find them individual enough. They all reminded Linda of her own mother, people who built walls and created **stereotypes** to **pigeonhole** other people in order to accommodate their own limited expectations. To Linda, such people were simply a reflection of the shallowness of all those whom they **emulated**, whether **peers** in school or the one-dimensional characters on television night-time soap-operas and situation comedies.

Danny had been the first boy she had ever met who **selflessly** demonstrated individual skill and daring rather than **submissively** allow himself to follow the path of **mindless obsequiousness**.

Linda knew he had thoughtfully conceived a uniquely daring plan to help a friend in need, executed it **flawlessly** and to **fruition**, yet asked nothing in return for his assistance. In her eyes, he was a warrior, a hero and, above all, a **compassionate** human being.

"I don't understand teachers, Jeremy. They are more interested in their books than they are in their students."

"I'm not sure they're even interested in their books, Linda," I added as we sat down upon one of the outside school benches, the Hawaiian summer sun shining brightly overhead.

"You're right, Jeremy. I can remember so many things my mom has said about her classes. You'd think she was a warden in the penitentiary."

"What kind of things?" I inquired.

"Oh, stuff like 'Those idiots can't even read anymore' or 'I'll flunk everyone if I have to.' Things like that. Like she doesn't even try to know anybody's name or even think that maybe some students are really trying their best."

"Or maybe all the students are," I added.

"That's the point. Everyone is trying to do their best. But my mom can't see that. She's burned herself out from years of repetition, and she's created a stale learning environment as a result."

"But what can she do?" I asked, **endeavoring** to display **empathy** for her mother's **plight** and for all teachers in the same situation.

"Jeremy, you know what they can do. You've said so yourself. They can become interested in what they're doing. They can read the books they teach and they can figure out ways to make the books interesting for each student. And if the books are old and boring, then they should get rid of the books and teach from experience. Nobody ever said that books are the only way to learn. They help, but they aren't everything. And most teachers don't know that. They think their job is to give out assignments **dictated** by books, created by books, taught by books. But why do we need teachers if books give us all the answers?"

I let her continue. Her words were soothing to my **psyche**, reflecting what I had tried to explain to Danny. He said I was a good teacher, and now I listened **intently** to hear what a good teacher really was, from a female voice of experience.

"Teachers are the soul of a school. They are the only ones who can make the future seem real, seem logical, seem **relevant** for everyone. It's a big bad world beyond, but with the teacher's guiding hand a student can make sense out of it. A student can walk out of high school secure that he or she knows what to do next, that what they learned from the books makes sense in today's world, not last century's. If it's from history, they should know that we need to avoid repeating the errors of the past, and if from math, that we need to know when we're being cheated at the supermarket. And from religion, that we should all live as brothers and sisters under the sun – sharing the same land and the same goals – and try to keep peace in the world. That's what school is supposed to teach. And that's why we need teachers, to show each individual person that it really does make sense to be in school, and not to simply flunk the whole class because a teacher feels like it. I'm sorry, but I don't see eye to eye with my mom when it comes to education. I might want to one day become a teacher just so I can try to change the way things are in school, but one person can only do so much. I'll do all I can, and that's about the best I can offer to the world." Linda leaned back against the bench, her **jeremiad** now complete and her thoughts drifting into the heavens beyond. She would indeed become an excellent teacher if one day she chose to fight against a system that disapproves of change. She and Mr. Osmar...and me.

CHAPTER XXI
A Contrast Of Control

With the **academic** school year officially over, I sought desperately to make contact with Danny, whom I hadn't heard from all week. I tried to contact him through my **cohorts**, but no one had seen him around. His mom had made it clear to me that my presence wasn't welcome, but I braved the waters and phoned one last time. The voice on the other side was just as **curt**.

"I told you not to call. I don't want anyone from school to call him." She then hung up, and I listened for a few seconds to the sound of silence before hanging up on my end. Danny was out of reach. I had no way of helping him now. I found myself **inescapably resigned** to await the moment when he would contact me.

☆ ☆

The Junior prom was held, as scheduled, on Saturday, May 16th. The 4:30 p.m. bus to took me to Linda, who lived on the other side of town three or four miles away in a **quaint** two-story duplex with her mom and dad. Being an only child, she was **afforded** great respect and **unfettered latitude**. Her mother obviously did not think of her as a "student" or else she'd never have been allowed to become such an independent individual.

Linda was waiting for me on her front steps. Dressed in informal **attire** with low-top shoes, she appeared very natural – not made-up or **gaudy** in any way. She dressed in good taste, and I knew her mother had no hand in her choice of clothes.

"Let's go, Jeremy, before my mom gets home," Linda urged. "She's shopping and I don't want to hear her silly advice." We departed hurriedly in the direction of the school, walking in the warmth of the late-afternoon sun to another bus stop farther away from her house.

The trees were in full bloom: mangoes dangled from outstretched branches of the lush trees; coconuts wavered high above from thin trees hardly able to support the weight; and an occasional lychee tree appeared, **replete** with **delectable** bite-sized lychee-nut **morsels**. I was tempted to pick from a low-hanging mango branch and hurl the one-pound fruit into the air, but I realized almost instantly that such childishness really had no place in a high-schoolers' life. We had come a long way through school to at least realize that such actions created no benefit in and of themselves, and that even if nothing were hit – even if no **malice** were intended – the event would gain no material satisfaction, no real advantage. It would be just for fun, but I didn't feel it would be appropriate while walking to the Junior prom with one's date.

As we approached one branch and both bowed our heads to avoid bumping heads with the fruits, Linda suddenly reached out, grabbed a mango and hurled it skyward. It returned to earth and crashed upon the street with a dull squashy thud.

Linda suddenly reached out, grabbed a mango and hurled it skyward.

"Gee, I've always wanted to do that," she said in typical *Doris Day* **glee**. "Sorry if I scared you, Jeremy."

I grinned from ear to ear, realizing that people don't really change. Not unless they choose to.

CHAPTER XXII
The Prom

The Junior prom was held in the heart of Waikiki, as was customary for each of the dozen different high schools in the Honolulu District. This year, the site selected was the *Waikiki Troubador Hotel*, with its massive corridors and ballrooms. The school had changed locations from last year after the vat-incident left the school **liable** for repairing the floors and wallpaper. Both school and hotel management were eager to avoid a **recurring** scene, and thus the *Troubador* – with its tighter security – became the more suitable setting.

Neither Danny nor Sarah was at the prom. Sarah was undoubtedly thousands of miles away, leaving Danny with little if any reason to appear. I felt a **twinge** of **nostalgic melancholy**, aware how much more special this day could be if only my best friend were here to share the magic with. But there was nothing I could do to change what had occurred and felt it out of place to display a **dolorous deportment** in front of Linda, for whom this day was also special.

As the daylight hours gave way to the **gloaming**, we **partook** in a **lavish** and **sumptuous** meal, after which Linda and I danced together and chatted about school, about our exams, and about our future plans as Juniors. Finally, our conversation turned to Danny and Sarah.

"How come Sarah couldn't stay?" I asked, hoping Linda had discovered more than I had about the incident.

"Her father told me that he had a very good job opportunity and that he would be there for at least three years. That was apparently the length of the contract. I asked him if Sarah might be able to stay, that she could stay with me, but it was really no use. After all, she's only going to be a Sophomore, and that means she's got three more years of school. How could I expect her father to seriously consider having her stay here?"

"What did Sarah say about all this? She hardly said a word of it to me."

"You know she was heartbroken. She loved Danny like a brother, even more perhaps. I guess she didn't know how to react to the separation. I told her that he'd wait for her if she wanted to one day come back to the islands, but it was just too long; and besides, she said, she couldn't let him hang on like that. That's why she tried to avoid talking about it. She was afraid she'd drag Danny into waiting for an eternity. And you know what happens after a while – people meet new friends. I knew she was right. There was no reason to **prolong** the **agony**. That's why I told you to stick close to Danny."

"Yeah, but his mom stopped me. I haven't seen him or heard from him in almost two weeks."

"Well, all we can do now is wait. I told Sarah to write as soon as she got to her new home in Atlanta. Maybe the letter will help ease the pain a bit. I gave her my address. I'll give you the letter when I receive it."

So at long last, I had learned about the details regarding the separation. Linda was truly thoughtful in encouraging Sarah to write so she could share the news with Danny. And yet, there was little anyone could do to keep the two together, given the distances in both time and place. Danny and Sarah wouldn't be seeing each other again for a long time – not until they were much older – if at all.

Linda and I remained together throughout the prom, hardly catching the eye of any of the other students. We were each loners in our own right, and together we enjoyed the early evening unbothered and in **solitary** innocence.

☆ ☆

The annual prom dance was being held this year at Campbell Auditorium – the largest building at Saint Paul School – where three rock bands were scheduled for an evening of summertime excitement. Linda and I arrived on campus just as the first band, the Rockets, started to perform some of their original heavy-metal rock. The second band would be more mellow, we were told, and the final hour would be solid '60s gold performed by Ace Cool and the Collectors. The evening was structured to start off with a bang and then slow down **progressively** into an evening of **retrospective** remembrance. For the students, much of the Collectors' music would be from a **bygone** era, though with the likes of *Animal House, Stand By Me* and *American Graffiti*, as well as the many television commercials for '60s rock-albums, we all expected to be somewhat familiar with at least half the songs. They would mark the beginning of a new age – new memories and new experiences to reflect upon in future years. Every song would **retain** its own magical moment, its own place in the sun. Whether or not the music would bring back memories for the teachers mattered little; this dance was for the students to enjoy – this was our evening to express ourselves.

During the evening, many of my school acquaintances stopped by to say hello and to inquire about Danny. Mr. Salvo had apparently been so overwhelmed by the outburst **levied** against him that he threatened the class he would resign if the students didn't shape up, and one student in his class told me they applauded and cheered the possibility. Danny may have been expelled, but he wasn't the only one who apparently felt the effects of the **tumultuous hullabaloo**.

Mr. Osmar also dropped by to wish me a happy and memorable evening as well as the best of everything in my Junior year. He added his **condolences** for Danny, explaining that the system fails when it can't support its youth. He had come with his wife and two young boys and was one of the adult chaperones attending the dance, probably one of the very few who volunteered to be there.

Linda and I exchanged our *Alohas* to the two kids, each around five or six years old. "And what do you want to be when you grow up?" I asked the slightly taller of the two.

Mr. Osmar had come with his wife and two young boys...

He looked at me with his big, round blue eyes and said "My daddy." Linda and I looked at each other, surprised and amused.

"Well, you sure have a daddy to be proud of," I replied. "Maybe one day you'll be just like him."

I wondered how many students could honestly say they'd want to be like their parents when they grew up. Mr. Osmar wasn't a teacher just in school; he was also a teacher at home. 'Teacher' was not a bad word when applied to Mr. Osmar, for he really knew how to help make learning a meaningful experience, and it showed in his own children. They were intelligent, bright-eyed and happy, just like the students in his classes. He stood in front of me as an adult, but he meant much more. More than an adult, more than a parent. He symbolized everything positive about humanity. He was the **epitome** of sharing, caring and loving. Here was a person I was proud to call a teacher.

"Well, you two kids take care of yourselves," Mr. Osmar continued, "and don't do anything I wouldn't do. Or if you do, don't tell anyone!" He then took his leave with his family, Linda and I holding hands and smiling at his light-heartedly suggestive words of advice. He was able to make everyone feel comfortable and in good humor with but a few words of kindness. No other teacher I knew possessed such a trait of **unfeigned** human warmth.

The heavy metal Rockets concluded their **stint** as the second band, the Waikiki Casuals, began a set of **dulcet** and **melodious** Hawaiian tunes. The stage was set for slow dancing. Linda and I had the chance to show everyone how close we were, but she saw through the **artifice** and elected to stay on the sidelines.

"Jeremy, I like to dance, but not while everyone's watching. That's the trouble with dances; they are just too crowded. I'm not sure after a while if we're dancing or just trying to keep from being stepped on or kicked. Somehow I don't fit very well in these large social gatherings. Maybe I'm just a bit weird."

"You're just a little bit individual, that's all. And I bet everyone else wishes they could be alone with their date and not herded together like this."

"You really think so?" Linda asked. "I don't really think so. You'd be surprised how many people like to be told what to do, how to act, when to love and when to hate."

I reflected briefly on the Panthers – the pack of **mindless** followers – and realized just how perceptive Linda was. The **unmitigated veracity** of her **dispassionate** words could not be **refuted**.

"Shall we dance anyway?" I responded. "After all, are we going to let a bunch of followers stop us from doing what we want to do?"

"Okay, maybe a few dances." She understood my meaning. There was no reason to shy away from doing what we wanted on account of a crowd. We could probably find just as much satisfaction dancing out in the moonlight by ourselves, but I wanted to experience the thrill and the glory of sharing at least a few memories with Linda on the school dance-floor.

The evening event progressed in characteristic high-school fashion, with more socializing than dancing – a few minor clashes between **rivals**, but mostly meetings amongst friends and casual acquaintances. The teachers strolled around the perimeter, watching out for anything illegal that might find its way into the auditorium. The exit doors were kept closed to prevent "undesirables" from entering as well as to keep the noise from **antagonizing** the neighborhood, which had argued in the past against such activities in the later evening hours.

As the Casuals closed out their performance, the Collectors began to assemble their instruments and light show. Within a few short minutes the entire room was transformed into a '60s sock-hop. The mood changed completely as *Little Darlin'* and *Peggy Sue* rocked the hall. The mood was **upbeat** and everyone was dancing. Even Linda and I couldn't resist the beat.

"If this is what music was like in the '60s," she began, "then I wish I had a time-machine. This is really great stuff."

The dance-marathon continued right through the evening, no one aware of the fire that had begun two buildings away.

CHAPTER XXIII
A Hazy Nightmare

The smoke came from Miller's Annex, beginning as a small flame and quickly turning into a **raging** chemical fire as it reached the neighboring room which housed books, films and cleaning materials, agents highly flammable and **combustible**. Although accompanied by loud explosions from within the closed doors of the Annex, the sounds of the **incendiary** blaze were **muted** by the music of the Collectors. But the smoke **billowed** as the fire roared through the Annex building, then leaped to the neighboring Sussman Student Center and rapidly made its descent upon Campbell Auditorium.

Students were dancing heatedly to *Rock Around the Clock* when the first traces of smoke entered through the ceiling fan system. Within a minute, there was **frenetic bedlam** as fumes attacked from every port of entry. The electrical lines were melted by the heat almost immediately, sending students and teachers alike tumbling in darkness to the floor, searching **frantically** for the exits.

The sound of screams was **deafening**. Linda and I kept our hands clasped tightly together as we **groped** for an exit, managing to reach the closest one but discovering, along with a dozen others before us, that it had been blocked off. The front entrance door was then thrust wide open and one of the exit doors broken through by a **throng** of panic-stricken teens. Students piled out of the two doors, landing on the grass outside and catching their breath before continuing their **exodus**. Sirens of fire engines approached as Linda and I followed the crowds through the open exit, gasping for air and then resuming our path in a drunken manner, hand-in-hand, towards the open grounds. The football field quickly filled up with students coughing and screaming and crying. We all watched in horrified shock as the auditorium belched smoke into the air, then suddenly began to **illuminate** as though **radiated** by a **resplendent** spotlight. Though metal frames held the complex intact, the wooden walls and floors ignited **simultaneously** with an **intensity** unimaginable, pouring forth **caustic** clouds of heat which **singed** the adjacent grass and caused a burning sensation in our eyes as we watched. In another minute, the three buildings were mere hollow shells supported only by the fire-resistant frames.

Within ten minutes the **conflagration** was under control, ambulances were arriving from neighboring hospitals, and doctors and nurses tended to the injured and those overcome by **toxic** fumes. Linda and I stayed together, still hand-in-hand, refusing treatment. We were uninjured.

The next couple of hours passed like a hazy dream – a timeless, foggy fantasy. Nobody was certain what had happened, who had been hurt, and if anyone was trapped inside. Parents began arriving from all directions but were halted by the police, who had **cordoned** off the area to allow medical personnel to enter and exit. Those students who chose to leave for home wandered away in disbelief, but most stayed behind, sitting on the grass in a **lugubrious** and **funereal** silence, observing the remains of what had been the site of the dance just a short time earlier.

Students piled out of the two doors, landing on the grass outside before continuing their exodus.

I heard the mention of Miller's Annex, whereupon my immediate association was with the Striped Panthers. Instinctive fear drove me to my feet and in the direction of the Annex, Linda and I parting hands.

"No, I want to go too," she said emotionally, rising and following behind me as we made our way toward the **residual plumes**.

As we neared the Annex, following the spotlights of the fire department, I interrupted one of the firemen. "How did the whole thing start?" I **implored**.

"Down in that building," and he pointed to the area where the Panthers held their monthly meetings. "Looks like paint and oil. But I'm not sure. I didn't think they stored that combination in schools."

Linda and I had **concurrent** suspicions. Danny.

"Did you get to see if anybody might have been in there?" I continued.

"Why do you ask?" the fireman responded. "You think somebody was in there?"

"I don't know," I answered immediately. "I don't think so, but that was the meeting-room for a school-club, and maybe someone was working there or something." I didn't wish to waste words explaining what I really believed had happened; I was only interested in knowing whether anyone had been in the room.

"Look, son, I don't know. Read about in it tomorrow's paper, okay. I've got a lot of work to do, and nobody's going into that building for a few hours. Much too dangerous – look at those walls."

The sides of the Annex clung together like shaky wires ready to collapse, and I could see that nothing would be revealed until daybreak. I took Linda's hand and we walked away from the scene of the **devastation**.

"Osmar's dead," someone exclaimed, running by us in the darkness. Linda and I stopped still. The words pounded against me like an anvil being dropped on my head. I couldn't think. Everything seemed to change directions. The cars in front of me suddenly grew large, then small, then large again. My head began to split into pieces. I stared down at the soft grass below, which suddenly moved closer and closer. I could feel myself falling, the grass rising. My body was losing strength, and as I saw myself dropping helplessly to the ground, all I could think of were two young boys whose father was named Osmar. The boys looked familiar. I could see their faces. One was Danny, the other was me. Then all went black.

CHAPTER XXIV
The Discovery

I regained consciousness the next morning at *Kaiser Hospital* to find Linda Kilbraith standing with my parents by my side.

"Did it really happen?" I asked, praying that it was all just a dream.

Linda showed me the front-page headlines, and I knew it had all really happened. I gazed upon the story as though reading about my own life flashing before my eyes.

**SCHOOL FIRE KILLS TEACHER,
INJURES 41 STUDENTS**

(Honolulu)--A spectacular fire roared through a local high school, killing one person and injuring 41 others.

According to firemen on the scene, the fire started in a neighboring basement and soon **engulfed** the school auditorium, where a summer dance was being held. Over 250 students from Saint Paul School fled to safety through the only two exits which were open. Fire marshals indicated that safety violations had occurred which may have contributed to the extent of injuries.

Cause of the fire is under investigation, although **arson** has not been ruled out. According to one eyewitness, a sudden explosion erupted in Miller's Annex, two buildings away from Campbell Auditorium, scene of the summer dance attended by Sophomores and Juniors from Saint Paul School. The explosion was soon followed by a chemical fire fueled by what appeared to be "highly **inflammable concoctions**," as one rescue official termed it.

Within three minutes, the auditorium was in flames. Although fire rescue arrived four minutes later, the blaze took three hours to contain. Six fire trucks helped to extinguish the fire.

The lone casualty was Mr. Herman Osmar, English teacher at Saint Paul School, who apparently stayed behind to help others escape the burning building. One observer called his actions "the bravest thing I've ever seen." Osmar, 37, had been a teacher at Saint Paul School for 8 years. He is survived by his wife and two sons, who also attended the dance. They were not injured.

Those requiring further medical assistance were taken to nearby hospitals, and all except four have been released. The four are reported in good condition and are expected to be released shortly.

Police have refused to speculate on the cause, citing instead several **improprieties** discovered at the scene: blocked fire exits, inadequate teacher supervision and a possibly faulty sprinkler-system.

Father Eugene Conquistador, Principal of Saint Paul School, was unavailable for comment. His secretary said, however, that the matter would be looked into and that school officials would assist in police efforts to locate the cause of the fire to **ensure** that such a blaze could never happen again.

I looked up at my parents and at Linda, who waited patiently for me to finish reading the article.

"You made it into the front page, Jeremy," Linda said softly with a smile, referring obviously to the mention of the four students still hospitalized.

"Do you think it was...?" I left the question open-ended. Linda understood the reference.

"I don't know. I wish I could say 'No', but I really don't know."

I cupped my hands over my face, trying to place all the events into proper perspective. Mr. Osmar was dead. My favorite teacher was dead. His two young boys had no father. The best teacher in the entire school would never return. He had loved the summer so much; it was **ironic**. Bitterly **ironic**.

My thoughts then drifted to Danny. The blocked exits, the "paint and oil," it all sounded too much like Danny. And Miller's Annex. It was too coincidental. It had Danny's **M.O.** written all over it.

"Do you think it was...?" I left the question open-ended.

I took my hands away from my face and stared up against the **sterile** walls of the hospital room. The walls held no secrets. There was nothing more for me to discover here. I closed my eyes and went into a deep, deep sleep.

☆ ☆

I awoke in a world of dream. Danny and I were lying in the sands of Waikiki, tanning ourselves under the watchful rays of the **benevolent** sun. We were kids again, sharing our finest moments together. Everyone around us seemed to sense that the day was meant for us, as though they all simply contributed to our happiness, our security. Danny's hazel whites **glimmered** in the noontime **radiance**, reflecting the soft white **billowy** waves that approached us from **afar** as though **servilely** crawling to our feet, laying their gifts before us, then returning to the sea from **whence** they came.

Nearby, a transistor radio sang for us, **bestowing** upon us all the blessings of supportiveness and acceptance:

> *"Keep smiling, keep shining knowing you can always count on me,*
> *For sure, that's what friends are for;*
> *In good times, in bad times, I'll be at your side forevermore,*
> *That's what friends are for."*

I could see myself turn to one side, face Danny and say, beaming, "Yeah, that's what friends are for." Danny smiled back, then added, "We're the best. Everything's here for you and for me, pal. Yeah, it's great to be young, free and happy."

We then got up from the sand – slowly stroking our bodies to remove the sand that had **adhered** to our skin – and showed off our thin, attractively youthful bodies to all the admiring adults who watched in envy.

"Martha, I wish I could be young like that again," one of the tourist sunbathers said **wistfully** to his wife as he viewed us appreciatively.

Danny and I dug our feet into the sand, taking each step **deliberately** and in adolescent *Adonis* fashion, **mindful** of all the eyes upon us.

The **azure** waters **beckoned** us to enter and enjoy its warm, **caressing** waves – its gift to eternal youth – and as we let the stimulating salty spray blow **enticingly** against our faces, we waded **majestically** into the playful island sea.

We **frolicked** under the **effulgence** of our guiding sun, applauding each wave that one another body-surfed to shore, yelling in childish **glee**, **cherishing** every moment that life granted us.

121

And once we had exhausted ourselves in **mirth** and merriment, we put an arm around one another's shoulder and galloped like young stallions back to our private beach.

"Danny," I asked, "what's life all about?"

"It's for having fun. It's for being young. It's for sharing with your friends. That's what life is all about."

Danny had revealed the secret. One could ask for nothing more, be truly satisfied with nothing less. All that we had lived for brought us to this moment of innocence, and no deeper meaning in life would ever be necessary. We had become immortalized, forever an impression upon the sands of time.

Then I heard another tune in the background which brought my dream closer to reality:

"Oh yeah, life goes on
Long after the thrill of living is gone;
Oh yeah, I said life goes on
Long after the thrill of living is gone..."

and I could see Danny, a proud teenager standing alone, watching the world from high atop an apartment balcony. He was gazing **pensively** at the sky, the mountainside, and then below at the people walking by, lost in crowds, each one seeking identity in a world of **conformity**. His golden bronze skin hid his inner **torment**, an **anguish accrued** over years of misunderstanding and **degradation**. His **embryonic** innocence had been **withered** away by **malefic**, **pernicious** words of hate and destruction cast upon him by those who secretly envied his youth: parents and teachers and others jealous of his independence and of his self-directed will for survival. They joined forces to defeat him, to reform him, to make him become one of them: a broken, tired, **mindless** soul.

But they hadn't broken him. He was still the angel of light, wrinkled somewhat under the eyes from the tears he shed, but yet still free. Misunderstood but free.

Danny stood alone, high above the world, then suddenly climbed atop the balcony railing, gazed **longingly** at the heavens above, and leaped out to meet his fate.

☆ ☆

I jumped up from my hospital bed, shaking my head wildly to remove the image from my mind. Danny was dead. Danny was dead. I couldn't accept it. Was Danny really dead?

I grabbed a shirt and dashed out of the hospital room; nobody was in the room to stop me. Maybe they were still there, but I couldn't see them. I ran and ran and ran in my shirt and pajamas towards the school that bore the truth.

122

We frolicked under the effulgence of our guiding sun... cherishing every moment that life granted us.

He was still the angel of light, wrinkled somewhat under the eyes from the tears he shed, but yet still free.

123

Time passed without meaning. It was morning, but I didn't know exactly what time; it didn't matter. I kept running, my breath short and my mind weary. But I kept running, running wildly toward what lay there for me to witness.

After an **interminable** journey I could see the school approaching. No one had stopped me, nothing could stop me. I was still in my dream, but I knew this was real. My mind saw Danny, but my eyes saw the school grounds directly ahead, still **cordoned** off with ropes. I flew madly past them and landed outside of Miller's Annex. I stopped. I awoke. I was there.

"Can I help you, son?" the watchman asked.

"No," I answered automatically. "I just need to go inside that room, mister."

"But there's nothing left. Just **rubble**."

"I've gotta look inside," I echoed **robotically**.

"Go ahead then, son. Hope you find what you're looking for."

I walked slowly but alertly into the **rubble**, the three-story **edifice** that now resembled three levels of an empty shell. The Annex contents lay visibly scattered along the floor. Pieces of **charred** wood and several large cans littered the area, the last **vestiges** of the carefully planned scheme, the ultimate form of expression. Everybody had heard. People were injured, Mr. Osmar was dead. But I couldn't find fault with the idea. My own words haunted me: 'You were right in what you did. I don't know if they were the best-laid plans, but nobody has the right to put you down for taking a stand and acting on it. That's between a person and his conscience, nobody else.' And then the **cryptically apocalyptic** response from Danny spoke to me from the ashes below: 'I think you're right, Jeremy. I think a person's got to speak up for what he believes, even if it kills him. Sometimes the truth is too powerful to hide. It's like something deep inside that's gotta come out.'

I bowed my head and let the tears flow **uninhibitedly** to the ground below. The tears were for Danny, but they were tears of joy, not sorrow. Danny had discovered the truth and had not sold himself short. He had a message for everyone, and nobody could stop him from saying it. Not Salvo, not Saint Paul, not his mom, not even me. He was free at last.

CHAPTER XXV
Reflections

Yes, the newspapers were wrong. Nobody really knew the truth, nobody but Danny and me.

Saint Paul never associated Danny with the fire. And if they had discovered evidence that someone was in the building, they never exposed the truth. They were more interested in preserving their **untarnished** image, their **self-righteous** system.

I learned a bitter lesson about life, a lesson Dr. Wong had shown to me three years before: If you don't learn to compromise in life, you'll lose it all in the end. But Dr. Wong wasn't completely right, because Danny didn't lose it all. He only lost the battle; he won the war. He took bold actions while I could not face up to them. He made the system listen to him, while I merely complained and **conformed** to it. But when he lit the fuse and set the school ablaze, I was there with him. We didn't compromise then. And we won. We won together.

☆ ☆

The former auditorium was restored within three months in an attempt to **whitewash** and **downplay** the **nocturnal** nightmare. No one was ever blamed, nothing more was said about the fire. And as for Danny, rumors spread that he left his parents' house and boarded a plane for the Mainland. I never contested the story. It would have accomplished nothing. Nobody would have listened. Nobody would have understood. And even if they had, what proof could I offer? Could I even convince myself? Was Danny really dead, or were the rumors perhaps true?

I never revealed my suspicions to anyone except Linda. We waited together, hoping to hear from our friend or receive confirmation that he had indeed been a victim in the school blaze. But word never came.

My Junior year began, but still no word from Danny. I had become the newspaper editor and was asked to provide a plaque for the newly reconstructed Osmar Auditorium, renamed in honor of the **venerated** teacher who lost his life in an effort of heroism. I **labored** long hours to write something that would in some **subtle**, personal way reflect what Danny and Mr. Osmar would have wanted to say. The short poem was submitted and **readily** accepted, though the school plaque-committee found the words **elusive** and **enigmatic**.

During the dedication ceremony, the plaque was mounted on the wall while students and faculty watched. And as I read the inscription aloud, I could feel the grounds echo in approval for the words that would survive throughout eternity, words that refused to **conform** or compromise, words that spoke for Danny, for Mr. Osmar, for Linda, for Sarah, for me, for all the students at Saint Paul School:

FEAR NONE BUT THE INNOCENT
WHO INHERIT DREAMS FROM AN ANGRY WORLD
FEAR NONE BUT THE INNOCENT
WHEN THE FUTURE SHALL BE THEIRS TO RULE

I could feel the grounds echo in approval for the words that would survive throughout eternity...

FEAR NONE BUT THE INNOCENT
WHO INHERIT DREAMS FROM AN ANGRY WORLD;
FEAR NONE BUT THE INNOCENT
WHEN THE FUTURE SHALL BE THEIRS TO RULE.

I offered this saying for everyone who has ever felt that we need to reevaluate ourselves and our systems, for everyone who, like Danny, has suffered from a world gone mad, a world in which even the family unit seems to have become little more than a box of *Rice Krispies*.

END

THEME SONG
Fear None But The Innocent
Lyrics by Raymond Karelitz

As we looked up at the world with newborn eyes,
We saw the world in clearest true blue skies;

Then as the years crawled by and times they changed,
We saw a need in us to rearrange.

And what we saw from far behind the dreams
Was reality: the systems and the schemes.

FEAR NONE BUT THE INNOCENT
WHO INHERIT DREAMS FROM AN ANGRY WORLD;

FEAR NONE BUT THE INNOCENT
WHEN THE FUTURE SHALL BE THEIRS TO RULE.

We grew, we dreamed, we learned, we schemed untold,
But youth did not find way to change the old;

And as they forced us more to compromise,
We discovered their deceit, their hurt, their lies.

Soon, fearing change in us, we tried to flee
But conflicts grew and tore our fantasy.

FEAR NONE BUT THE INNOCENT
WHO INHERIT DREAMS FROM AN ANGRY WORLD;

FEAR NONE BUT THE INNOCENT
WHEN THE FUTURE SHALL BE THEIRS TO RULE.

We've seen, we've learned the lies that we were told
But in our hearts we know it isn't so;

And as we travel on, we won't forget
The dreams and fantasies that we first met.

And yes, one day the world will hear youth's call
When the refrain echoes far beyond our halls:

FEAR NONE BUT THE INNOCENT
WHO INHERIT DREAMS FROM AN ANGRY WORLD;

FEAR NONE BUT THE INNOCENT
WHEN THE FUTURE SHALL BE OURS TO RULE.

Fear None But The Innocent
Glossary

The following words (deemed by the editor to be of challenging difficulty and of particular value in college writing and in entrance exams such as the S.A.T.) appear in this novel. Each word is then defined briefly in its context.

You are encouraged to purchase a marking-pen which accentuates text, highlight unfamiliar key words as they appear, and complete the highlighting process by accentuating the glossary-definition of the word.

This process of word-building through reading and highlighting will not only help you add to your vocabulary, but it will also help introduce you to the highly effective method of highlighting for future readings as well!

Glossary
Fear None But The Innocent

abettor (40) assistant in crime

absentia (48) see **in absentia**

academic (30, 33, 58, 60, 78, 101, 104, 107) intellectual

accede (49) give in

accentuated (48) give emphasis to / mark with emphasis

access (67) entry

acclaimed (73) praised

accomplice (38) helper in crime

according (49) granting

accrued (122) accumulated

acquiesce (29, 44) give in quietly

acquisition (30) acquiring

acute (36) sharp

adapted (17) adjusted

addled (27) confused

adeptly (70) expertly

adhere (121) stick

adieu (66, 84) goodbye

adjutant (30) assistant

ado (82) bustling activity / commotion

adolescent (121) youthful

Adonis (121) [Greek Mythology] a handsome youth

adoration (34) worship

adversity (46, 58) misfortune

afar (54, 61, 121) a distance

affected (67) artificial

affective (100) emotional

affirm (38, 54, 78) confirm

afforded (14, 19, 46, 53, 82, 107) provided

agony (110) pain and distress

air (67) manner

akin (21) related / similar

alas (14, 103) (loosely) too bad

allay (56) calm

allegations (43) charges

alluding (56) referring indirectly

ally (35) friend and associate

Alohas (111) [Hawaiian] greetings

alterations (30, 101) changes

alumni (14) graduates

amassed (48) accumulated

ambience (32) atmosphere

ambivalently (60) undecidedly

amicably (84) friendly and peaceably

amity (29) friendly relations

amply (86) adequately

analogous (17) comparable

anarchy (58) confusion and disorder

anathema (32) a thing cursed

androids (32) robots

angelic (30, 56) like an angel

anguish (122) distress

animosity (18, 29) bitter resentment

antagonizing (114) arousing the hostility of

anthropomorphic (32) given human characteristics to

antics (2, 32) mischievous deeds

apathetically (15) indifferently

apocalyptic (124) expressing a revelation or message

appeased (71) satisfied

appellations (48) names

apprehension (66) fearful uneasiness

aptly (74) suitably / appropriately

arctic (15) freezing

array (32) orderly arrangement

arrogance (51) unwarranted show of pride and superiority

arson (118) malicious fire-setting

artful (3) clever and tricky

artifice (113) clever scheme

ascertain (84) establish

asinine (2) silly / stupid

aspirations (53, 86) ambitions / goals

assayed (11) analyzed the worth of

assert (19, 53, 80) demonstrate forcefully

assertively (45, 100) positively and insistently / forcefully

assessing (60) evaluating

1

attain (29, 44, 53) accomplish

attentively (97) with concentrative attention

attire (51, 107) clothes

attributes (81) qualities / characteristics

audible (65) able to hear

aura (27) distinctive quality / distinctive atmosphere

auspicious (67) favorable

authenticating (82) establishing as genuine and reliable

autocratic (9) dictatorial

avail (103) benefit

avaricious (54) greedy

avenged (101) repaid (through an act of vengeance)

azure (121) clear blue

bacchanalian (14) drunken

baited (45) lured

bamboozled (4) tricked / deceived

banality (104) staleness

baneful (56) harmful

banished (35) expelled

barrage (42) overwhelming number / rapid outpouring

baseless (81) without merit

battery (43) group

beacon (33) guiding light

beatific (33) blissful

beaus (82) suitors / dates

beckoned (121) summoned / attracted

bedlam (115) chaos

befell (46) happened to

befriend (4, 30, 45) make friends with

beguiling (43) charming

belied (8, 66) misrepresented / showed differently than

bellowed (14) roared in a deep, loud tone

bemused (54) stunned / bewildered

beneficiary (49) person who benefits

benevolent (121) charitable

berate (50) scold

beseeching (80) begging

besieging (65) bombarding

besmirch (44) tarnish / soil

bespectacled (60) wearing spectacles (glasses)

bestowing (121) granting

bewilderment (54) confusion

billowed (115) swelled

billowy (121) massively surging and cloudlike

blared (84) sounded loudly

blasé (19) boring

blatant (6, 48, 91) clearly obvious

bleak (58, 67) gloomy

bliss (14) joy

blunt (81) abrupt /.insensitive

blustery (34) windy

boisterous (14) noisy and rowdy

bolster (18) support

bombast (93) pompous language

bravado (33) showy and daring display of courage

brazen (14) shamelessly bold

brouhaha (44) uproar

brusquely (27) rudely sudden and forceful

burgeoned (17) flourished

burrow (3) dig

bygone (111) past

calculating (44) scheming

callow (81) inexperienced / immature

camaraderie (74) close friendship

candor (27) honesty and directness

caper (40, 46, 101) wild escapade

capitulate (78) submit

capricious (104) changeable

caressing (121) gently touching

carte blanche (45) free reign

caustic (115) burning / stinging

caviling (61) finding fault / nitpicking

celestial (32, 84) heavenly

censor (87) evaluate (to omit undesirable elements)

cerebral (19) pertaining to the brain

chaos (53) turmoil

chaotic (49) confused

charlatan (103) fraud

charred (124) scorched

chartreuse (82) yellowish-green

chary (38) cautiously watchful

chastise (17) criticize severely

cherish (18, 24, 45, 121) hold dear

chicanery (14) trickery and deception

chide (17) scold mildly

chimerically (1) fancifully

chivalric (27) courteous and courageous

chivalry (33) chivalric code

chortled (11) chuckled and snorted

circumspect (40) careful

clamoring (4) crying out

clandestine (24) secret

clarion (60) clear

climacteric (54) critical period

climactic (80) decisive

clique (80) private group

coalesced (69) united

coalition (48) alliance or group

cogent (72) forcefully convincing

cogitating (60) pondering

cognizant (97) aware

cohorts (107) companions / associates

collaborate (21, 27, 58) work together

collectively (12, 35) together

combustible (115) able to catch fire and burn

comeliness (32) beauty

commemorated (82) honored the memory of / served as a memory

commenced (70, 82, 100) began

commonality (87) in common

compassion (9, 45) deep feeling of sharing and concern for another

compassionate (89, 105) kindhearted

compatible (29) in harmony

compatriot (53) colleague / fellow countryman / companion

compelled (67) driven / urged on

complacency (19) feeling of self-contentment

complexities (100) complications

complied (51) obeyed

compound (40, 67) magnify

comprised (104) consisting

compulsion (8) uncontrollable desire

comrade (34, 67) friend

conceded (11) acknowledged

conceptualize (56) envision

concerted (51) mutual

concoct (43) formulate

concoction (9, 118) creation

concurrent (117) occurring at the same time

condemnatory (6) criticizing

condescendingly (101) acting as if superior and lowering oneself to address another

condolences (111) expressions of sympathy for another's sorrow

condone (76) overlook / tolerate

conducive (49) contributing / leading

conferred (48) held a conference

confidante (1, 49, 93) (female) person confided in

confide (1, 46, 58, 61) reveal one's personal thoughts truthfully

conflagration (115) large and destructive fire

conform (125) obey / act in accordance

conformity (1, 63, 122) submission / obeying the rules

confrere (51) cohort / associate

confront (6, 60, 78, 93) challenge face to face (in battle)

confrontation (27, 71) battle / conflict; unfriendly encounter / face-to-face

connotation (38) deeper meaning

connoted (35) suggested (in a deeper sense)

consented (44) agreed to what was suggested

consolation (17, 91) comfort (to help ease grief)

conspirator (21) schemer

consternation (54) panic and fear

contemplate (1, 78, 91) consider deeply and seriously

contend (49) assert / argue in opposition

contrived (11) plotted

convalesced (21) recuperated

convened (45) began

converged (82) came together

conversed (24, 58) talked informally

convictions (101) beliefs

convivial (9, 37) sociable

coordinated (3) organized

copious (69) abundant

cordoned (115, 124) protectively restricted (with rope, cord or ribbon) / blockaded and enclosed

corporeal (100, 103) physical

cosmic (100) relating to the universe

countenance (8, 37, 99) outward (facial) appearance

coup (66) overthrow of the ruler

covert (12) hidden and secretive

crafted (48) produced skillfully

crass (81) crude

crossroads (60) critical point

crucial (86) important

crudely (32) vulgarly

crusades (32) idealistic missions

cryptically (124) puzzlingly

cue (14, 84) signal

culminated (54) climaxed

culprit (1, 42) guilty person

cunning (30) sly

curb (29) restrain

curricular (71) relating to courses of study

curt (91, 107) rudely brief

curtailed (34) cut short

damsel (34) see **fair damsel**

daredevil (11) recklessly adventurous

dauntlessly (46) courageously

de facto (9) actual

deafening (115) extremely loud

debacle (99) violent disruption

debased (38) degraded / shamed

debilitating (25) weakening

decadence (44) moral decay

decamped (44) fled

deceit (79, 103) deception or misrepresentation

deface (44) damage

defamatory (44) slanderous

deference (80) courteous respect

defiance (97) act of resistance

defiantly (101) in a boldly challenging manner

deficiency (3, 61) something inadequate

defied (100) challenged

deft (43) skillful

defuse (25, 81) make less tense / calm

degradation (37, 123) shame and humiliation

delectable (107) delicious

deliberate (60) careful in deciding / carefully considered

deliberately (121) slowly and carefully

delusions (51) false visions

demonically (11) devilishly

denigrating (9) slandering

deportment (110) conduct / behavior

derelict (14) abandoned

derogate (61) degrade

despicable (103) awful / disgraceful

despondent (96) depressed by loss of hope

detente (61) a relaxation of an otherwise tense situation

deter (6, 45) discourage / hold back

detonating (44) activating

detrimental (49) harmful

devastating (27, 36) overwhelming and destructive

devastation (117) total destruction

devised (38) planned

devoutly (11) devotedly / passionately

dialectic (71) logic

dialectics (78) systematic reasoning

diaphanous (100) sheer / translucent

dictated (105) determined / set forth

dictates (71) commands

didactic (71) instructional

dilated (100) expanded

dilemma (3, 56, 66, 73) difficult situation, problem or choice

diligently (73) in a hardworking manner

dire (81, 99) extreme

directive (103) order

disassociate (58) separate

discerning (93) distinguishing / identifying

discomfited (99) confused, dejected and embarrassed

discourse (37, 48, 101) conversation / communication

discreetly (48) carefully and prudently

discrete (33) separate

disintegrating (27) blowing apart into fragments

disparagement (65) belittling

dispassionate (113) objective

disportment (18) amusement / diversion

disposal (45) command

disquietude (53) state of uneasiness / agitation

disseminating (44) circulating

dissertation (71) lengthy written report

dissonant (97) clashing

distort (1, 99, 101) alter the meaning of

distracted (96) disturbed

distress (34) anxiety

divergent (64) different

diversionary (34) seeking to divert

divert (3, 91) distract

divine (32, 101) supremely good

divulge (35) reveal (as a secret)

docked (69) deducted (as a penalty)

dolorous (110) gloomy

Doris Day (109) movie actress in the 1950s and 1960s

doting (34) displaying excessive fondness

downplay (125) minimize

dreaded (66) feared

drudgery (24) boring monotony

dubiously (70) skeptically

dulcet (113) sweet-sounding

dyslexic (86) having a reading impairment

earnest (67) serious with sincere feeling

ebbed (87) declined

eclectic (32) diverse

edifice (124) building

effectuated (48) successfully accomplished

efficacy (48) effectiveness

effloresce (60) bloom

effulgence (121) radiance / brilliance

egregious (15) conspicuously bad

eked (out) (76) barely managed

elaborate (56, 81) explain in greater detail

elaborately (82) in a fancy and detailed manner

elicit (5) draw out / bring forth

elite (12, 101) members of a select group

elope (80) run away to wed secretly

eloquent (50) persuasive and effective manner of speech

elusive (125) hard to catch / difficult to understand

emanated (49) came forth

emblazon (21, 33) decorate in brilliant colors

emboldening (78) make bolder

embossed (82) raised

embryonic (122) underdeveloped

emergence (46) appearance / development

eminent (80) famous

empathy (105) compassion

emphatic (96) forceful

empyreal (32) heavenly

emulated (104) imitated (hoping to equal or surpass

enamored (34) amorous

enchantment (24) charm

encomium (34) praise

encompassing (33) containing

engendered (99) produced / gave life to

engrossed (30) deeply absorbed and interested

engulfed (4, 118) surrounded completely

enhance (12) intensify

enigmatic (125) mysterious and secretive

enlightenment (60) knowledge and truth and understanding

enlivened (1, 96) cheered up

enmeshed (57, 101) entangled / intertwined

ennui (19) boredom

enraptured (33) captivated

ensued (28) followed

ensure (12, 30, 43, 60, 119) guarantee

enterprise (67) undertaking

entertain (93) consider

enticingly (121) in a tempting manner

entities (32) beings

entree (82) admittance

entrenched (99) firmly

envisioned (32, 56) pictured in one's mind

ephemeral (104) transient / brief

epileptic (100) displayed by fits or seizures

epiphany (100) sudden revelation

epitome (61, 113) model / ideal representation

epitomized (11) represent ideally

equanimity (36) composure

escapades (4, 21) carefree, reckless adventures

eschewed (53) avoided

espied (10, 96) noticed / caught sight of

essence (24) essential substance

esteem (82) admiration / respect

ethereal (24, 32) heavenly

ethereally (100) light as air

euphemistically (19) in a polite and more socially acceptable manner

euphoric (74) blissful

eventuate (19, 56) result

evidenced (104) demonstrated

evocative (87) suggestive

exacting (38) strict and demanding

excursion (54) voyage

execrations (48) curses

executed (12, 19, 40, 48, 105) carried out

exhilarated (24) enlivened

exhilaration (38) cheerful excitement / feeling of excitement

exhorting (32) urging

exigency (35) emergency

exile (63) banishment

exodus (115) mass departure

expedient (78) self-serving

expletives (21, 78) profane "four-letter" words

exploit (42) feat

exploits (30) deeds or accomplishments / noteworthy feats

expulsion (58) ejection

extirpate (72) destroy completely

extracted (73) removed

extravagant (34) unrestrained / excessive

exultation (80) triumphant joyfulness

façade (51, 89, 101) superficial outward appearance / cover up

facility (74) ease

factions (48) groups

factious (101) causing unrest or ill will

fair damsel (34) see **fair maidens**

fair maidens (27) beautiful women

familial (9) family like

farcical (66) ridiculous

faux pas (71) blunder

fealty (66) loyalty

feasible (18) workable or manageable / able to be done or accomplished

feat (3) accomplishment

feigning (37) pretending

festered (81, 99) infected

fiasco (84) disastrous failure

fidelity (51) loyalty

filching (21) stealing

finale (99) conclusion

firmament (84) heavens

fixated (17) strongly attached

flatulent (51) pompous

flawlessly (84, 105) perfectly

fleeting (38) passing swiftly

florescence (34) state of flourishing

flourished (29) grew and prospered

foil (54) prevent the success of

folly (104) foolishness

foolhardy (15, 40) recklessly bold

foolproof (76) not capable of allowing error

foresee (71) see beforehand

forgo (71) do without or give up

formidable (12) fearfully impressive

fortuitous (30) unexpectedly lucky

fracas (21, 40) disorderly disturbance

frail (103) thin and weak

frank (27, 60, 87) honest and openly direct

frantically (115) excitedly

frenetic (115) frantic

frigid (12) extremely cold

frivolity (81) silliness / foolishness

frolicked (121) played in a happy, light-hearted manner

fruition (105) fulfillment

fugitive (104) runaway

funereal (115) gloomy

fury (12) rage / force

fusillade (58) barrage

futility (67) uselessness and hopelessness

galactic (32) concerning a galaxy (system of stars)

gaudy (107) showy in a tasteless manner

Gestapo (15) German secret police during WWII (in this context, implying "not to be argued with")

gist (72, 84) main idea or point

glacial (11) very cold

glee (109, 121) cheerfulness

glimmer (67, 121) flicker

gloaming (110) twilight

gloated (32) took great delight and satisfaction

goaded (19) spurred on or urged on

gossamer (31) thin / airy

grace (32) beauty and charm

grandeur (1, 51) greatness

grated (77) rubbed irritatingly

groped (115) searched blindly

grovel (2) crawl (as in a display of self-worthlessness

gullible (4) easily deceived or fooled

habituating (33) making accustomed

hackneyed (81) overused and unoriginal

hallowed (49) sacred

haphazard (69, 104) random / unplanned

hardy (32) rugged

harrowing (29) painfully disturbing

havoc (46) damage and commotion

head honcho (14) [slang] boss

headlong (71) recklessly and suddenly

heartening (76) encouraging

heartfelt (21, 84, 100) deeply felt / sincere

heeding (1) paying close attention

heinous (18) awful / disgraceful

heir apparent (44) next in line to rule

hematoma (19, 25) swelling

Hercules (100) mythical strong man

hitherto (11) until this time

hostilities (6, 61) acts of anger and unfriendliness

hover (27, 97) float above

hullabaloo (111) commotion

humiliation (35, 45) shame and disgrace

iconoclast (1) radical dissenter

ideology (60, 101) fundamental beliefs

idle (46) useless / meaningless

ill (54, 93) scarcely

illicit (50) not legal

illuminate (53, 115) glow

imbroglio (56) entanglement

imbued (38) filled or saturated / instilled

immaculate (32) spotless

immediacy (27, 103) urgent need

immerse (2, 46) involve deeply

imminent (32) happening soon

immobile (46) unable to move

impeccable (32) flawless

impelled (19, 45) urged forward / propelled

imperiously (15, 97) domineeringly

impetus (45) stimulus

implements (65) tools

implications (56, 73) involved consequences

implored (117) begged urgently

import (66) significance

imports (19) signifies

impressed (15, 44, 63, 76, 99) affect deeply / strongly

impressive (86) memorably striking

improprieties (119) mistakes

impugn (67) verbally attack

in absentia (48) in the absence of another

inane (3) silly and meaningless

inattentive (14) not observant or paying attention

inaugural (12) initial

incendiary (115) inflammatory

inchoate (48) unorganized

incipient (30) beginning

inciting (21, 53) provoking / arousing

inclement (34) stormy

incontrovertible (93) indisputable

incorrigible (61) delinquent

incredulous (11) skeptical and in disbelief

incriminating (4) involving one in a crime

inculcate (49, 60, 72) instill

indefatigable (6) tireless

indelible (8) permanent

indelicately (103) rudely

indifference (11, 37) unconcern / disinterest

indignation (35) resentment

indiscriminate (45) not selective

indoctrination (12) instructions

indolent (67) lazy

indomitable (18) unconquerable

inductees (15) people inducted

industrious (67) eagerly hardworking

ineffable (11) indescribable

ineffectual (49) without decisive effect / powerless

ineluctable (54) inescapable

inescapable (51, 107) unavoidable

inevitable (1, 48) inescapably unavoidable

inexorably (6, 67) relentlessly

inexpugnable (37) invincible

inextricably (44) hopelessly entangled

infallible (14, 38) without any fault or weakness / indestructible

infamous (15) known for bad deeds

infantile (15) childish

infectious (37) easily spreading

inferno (103) oven / fiery pit of hell

inflammable (118) burnable

infuse (19, 32, 100) inspire

ingenious (18) clever

ingenuous (18) naïve

inherently (101) naturally / innately

inimitable (56) unique

initiated (11, 44, 51) inducted

initiation (12, 44) formal entrance

injustice (45) wrong

innocuous (46) harmless

innuendos (101) indirect (usually negative) references and comments / hints and rumors

insatiable (53) unable to quench or satisfy

insidious (38) devious

insipidly (73) boring

instigated (14) provoked

insuperable (51) insurmountable

insurrection (60) outbreaks against authority

integral (54) essential

intensified (17) became more intense

intensity (66, 115) strength

intensive (29) concentrated

intent (38, 105) determined / insistent

interim (12) meantime

interjected (77, 81) inserted / added in

interminable (86, 124) exhaustingly endless

intermittent (97) recurring

interposed (84) interrupted / interjected intrusively

interrogated (9) formally questioned

interrogator (60) person interrogating

intervened (50) stepped in

intimate (46, 100) close and deeply personal

intonated (11) uttered

intricately (48) in a complicated manner

intrigued (44) fascinated

intuitive (32, 76, 86) natural, without need for deep thought / instinctive

inundated (17) flooded

invariably (6, 54) always

invective (65) abusive denunciation

inventive (48) skillfully original

inveterate (61) habitual

invincibility (11) unconquerability

inviolable (51) sacred

involuntarily (54) without choice

ire (35, 48) anger

irked (70) irritated

ironic (43, 73, 119) contrary to expectation / incongruous

irrefutable (53) undeniable

irreparably (96) irreversibly

irreproachability (32) absolute moral honor

irrespective (101) regardless

irrevocable (93) irreversible

jejune (32) immature

jeopardize (33, 77) put in danger (of loss)

jeremiad (106) mournful complaint

jest (11) humor / silliness

jocose (81) humorous

jollity (80) good humor

Judas Iscariot (103) [Bible] a traitor (generally)

justification (33, 67) answer

juvenile (33, 40) designated for minors

kaleidoscopic (100) constantly changing colors

kindle (21, 48, 87) fuel / arouse or excite

kindred spirit (103) close friend ("soul mate")

kinship (100) close relation

Knights of the Round Table (46) legendary court of King Arthur

labored (9, 125) struggled

laced (21) spiced up

lachrymose (87) sad / crying

lackeys (49) servile followers

lady fair (82) beautiful woman

lambasted (24) scolded severely

latitude (107) freedom of direction or action

latter (12) last

lavish (110) extravagant

leavening (91) lightening up

lest (48) for fear that

levied (14, 111) waged

liable (110) legally responsible

lineage (27) ancestral descent

litany (43) list

lithely (32) gracefully

loath (38) reluctant

loathe (21) hate

longingly (122) in a desiring manner

looming (71) hovering nearby

lovelorn (56) abandoned / jilted

lucid (46) clear-headed

lugubrious (115) gloomy

lunatic (25, 56) crazy person

M.O. (15, 119) see **modus operandi**

Machiavellian (49) deviously scheming

machinations (67) scheming / schemes

majestically (121) in a grand and royal manner

malcontents (87) people dissatisfied with conditions as they are

malefic (122) evil

malevolent (44) spiteful

malice (107) desire to injure or harm

malignant (12) malicious

maligned (16) slandered

manifest (29) exhibit

marginal (104) barely useful

martyr (99) person who suffers openly in behalf of a belief or a cause

mastermind (49) plan

materialize (1, 103) appear

maternalistic (8) motherly

matriarch (51) female ruler

maturation (2) growth into adulthood

maudlin (87) tearfully sentimental

maverick (60, 86) independent / apart from the herd

mawkish (3) excessively sentimental

mayhem (21, 49) wild, disorderly activity

meager (48) lacking fullness or richness

meddlesome (16) interfering and bothersome

mediocrity (67) state of being common and ordinary (not exciting) / unimpressive

mein kapitain (69) [German] my captain

melancholy (110) sadness

mélange (104) mixture

melodious (113) musical **memento** (54) souvenir or reminder of the past

memorialize (80) served as a memorial for

menacingly (32) threateningly

mendaciously (51) falsely

metamorphosis (32) complete change

metaphysical (32) transformational

methodically (40) systematically

meticulous (8) extremely careful and precise / carefully detailed

mien (8) manner

mindful (121) carefully watchful and aware

mindless (67, 104, 113, 122) unthinking

minions (67, 101) submissive followers / lower-class subjects

mirth (122) joy

misadventure (40) misfortune

misdeeds (48) malicious deeds

misguided (12, 60) misdirected

mock (17) imitating

modified (97) altered

modus operandi (M.O.) (12) method or style of doing things

momentous (80) extremely important

monolithic (51) massive

morality (38, 49, 101) conduct of good and bad behavior

morose (100) gloomy

Morse (Morse Code) (18) a system of communication using dots and dashes

morsel (49, 107) tiny piece

mortal (103) deadly

mortification (45) shame and humiliation

mortifying (40) embarrassing and shameful

mousily (56) timidly

muddled (25) jumbled and confused

mulling (over) (66) pondering

multifaceted (46) diverse

Glossary
Fear None But The Innocent

multitude (21) large number

mundane (100) day-to-day

mused (73) pondered at length

musketeers (21) armed soldiers

muster (15) assemble or gather together

muted (115) unable to speak / speechless

mutual (18, 48, 53, 86) shared

myriad (11, 46) numerous

mystique (44) mysterious qualities

naïvely (11) sincerely but without informed judgment

nascent (87) early-developing

necessitated (3) required

nefarious (33) evil

Nero (48) infamous Roman emperor

nocturnal (125) night time

nonchalant (1) cool and unconcerned

nonconformist (86) a person who refuses to go along with traditional customs

nonplussed (46) baffled / perplexed

nostalgic (110) remembering the past

notion (19, 44) idea / conception

notoriety (15) unfavorable reputation

nourish (33) promote and sustain

novel (37, 49) new and different

novices (19) newcomers

nugatory (73) worthless

nuptials (54) marriage

obfuscate (101) confuse

obligatory (45, 69) morally or legally required / mandatory

obliged (84) obligated

oblivion (32) state of being completely forgotten

obscene (15, 84) foul and offensive

obscured (12) hidden and unclear

obsequious (78, 104) submissive

obsolescent (73) becoming obsolete

odyssey (8) journey and experience

offensive (32, 73) insulting

ominously (12) threateningly

onslaught (32) violent attack

opining (103) expressing one's opinion

opportune (4) favorable or suitable / well-timed

oppression (11) cruelty

opprobrious (95) shameful

opted (24, 78) chose

optimistic (67, 96) positive and powerful

oracular (78) divinely revelatory

ostentation (93) showy display

ostentatious (35) extravagantly showy

otiose (73) purposeless / useless

outmoded (86) obsolete

overbearing (99) arrogant

palate (37) roof of the mouth

palpable (81) noticeable

panache (73) flair

pang (54, 66) sudden, sharp pain

pantheon (37) temple

paradox (63, 73) contradiction

paralytic (54) causing paralysis

paranoia (54) feelings of fear and distrust

pariah (35) social outcast

parochial (60) narrow-minded

partake (53) share

partook (110) shared

passé (33) obsolete

pathetically (6, 15) miserably pitiful

paucity (104) scarcity

pedagogical (60, 71) relating to teaching

pedagogy (104) teaching

pedantic (69, 71) relating to learning

peered (6) gazed intently / looked searchingly

peers (29, 53, 63, 99, 104) associates / fellow classmates

pejorative (48) insulting

penetrating (36) acutely insightful

pensively (122) dreamily and thoughtful

perceptively (10) keenly

percussion (56) impact

peremptory (103) absolute and without debate or argument

perennially (6) continually

perfidious (101) traitorous

perfunctory (58) halfhearted / unenthusiastic

perilous (40) hazardous

pernicious (122) injurious

perpetrate (14, 21, 48) commit

perpetrator (101) person who initiates an action

perpetuate (44, 60) prolong the existence of

perseveringly (18) persistently

persona (51) fictional character

personable (53) friendly

perspicacious (25) perceptive

perturbed (38) greatly disturbed

perverse (12) wrongheaded

petty (35) trivial

picaresque (46) adventuresome

picayune (71, 104) trivial / valueless

piddling (35) insignificant / measly

pigeonhole (104) stereotype

pilfering (18) stealing

pined (37) craved

piqued (14, 43, 72) aroused

pivotal (17) crucially important as a turning point

plague (36, 48, 100) torment

plenipotentiary (45) absolute / complete

plight (61, 67, 105) distressed and unfortunate situation

plumes (117) columns

plummeted (30) plunged downward

pomp and circumstance (104) ceremonious display

pompous (101) self-important

pondered (89, 101) considered carefully

potency (30) power

practicable (76) feasible / workable

prattle (32) foolish, silly talk

precarious (3) dangerous and insecure / risky

precinct (34, 42) patrolled neighborhood

predecessors (104) people who have preceded another

predestined (4) determined beforehand

predicament (35, 81) difficult, troublesome situation

predicated (103) based

predominant (14) dominant

prejudicedly (76) in a biased manner

premeditated (101) planned beforehand

premise (73) assumption

prerequisite (66) requirement

preside (84) govern

pretenses (38) artificial display

pretension (89) artificial or phony outward display

pretentious (101) boastfully showy

prevailing (18) prevalent

prevalent (82) widespread / widely existing

prime (17) primary

principal (16) main

pristine (32) pure and untouched

privy (49, 101) aware of a secret

probed (61) searched

problematic(al) (3, 18, 67) uncertain

prodding (35, 80) encouraging

proficient (18) skillful

profound (27, 36, 73) intense

progressively (111) continually advancing

prolong (110) extend

prominent (11) notable

pronounced (44) noticeable

prophetic (12) predicting

propinquity (33) nearness in time / relationship

propriety (69) conforming to the proper custom

prosaic (48) unimaginative

prostituting (63) selling out (to an unworthy cause)

protégé (66) person who is under the support and protection of another

proverbial (11, 73) relating to proverb / containing a practical message

provincial (71) narrow-minded

provocative (104) stimulating

provoke (48) stir or arouse

prowess (30) superior ability or skill

psyche (105) mind

psychic (6) supernaturally sensitive

pubescent (54) teenage / juvenile

puerile (2, 32, 42) childish

pulchritude (30) physical beauty

purging (101) cleansing

puritan (60) strictly and morally disciplined

purloined (43) stole

putrescent (66) decaying

quagmire (60) predicament

quaint (107) charmingly old-fashioned

qualms (53) misgivings

quandary (93) dilemma

quell (29, 66) subdue

queried (27, 67) questioned

quest (34) search

quid pro quo (45) returning a favor for a favor ("tit for tat")

quiescence (46) calm

quintessence (11) perfect embodiment

quip (91) remark in a witty manner

radiance (121) brilliance

radiated (24, 115) emitted

rage (56) violently, hostile anger

raging (115) violent

raillery (81) good natured teasing

rankle (46) irritate

rationale (24, 67, 72, 101) body of reasons supporting a belief

raucous (97) rough / harsh

readily (11, 29, 125) prompt and willingly

realize (2) accomplish

recalcitrant (11) stubbornly rebellious

receded (51) withdrew

recesses (97) inner parts

reciprocal (45) done in return

reckoned (42) dealt / settled

reckoning (14, 56, 71) final judgment or settlement

recounted (21, 65) narrated the facts of / related

recourse (6) option

recur (36, 110) occur again / continue repeatedly

redeeming (19) offset the bad effects of

redemption (33, 67) liberation from sin

redolent (65) reminiscent

refrained (69) held back

refuted (113) proven false

reign (15) rule

reinforce (18) strengthen

rekindle (30) reawaken / restart

relegated (30) assigned to a position of rank

relevant (71, 96, 105) appropriate

reliant (104) dependant

relished (77) enjoyed greatly

reminiscent (45) dealing with or concerning the past

remorseful (101) sad

renaissance (33) renewal / rebirth

rendezvous (69) prearranged meeting

renegade (77) deserter

repartee (65) witty conversation

repertoire (19, 65) complete list or storage

replete (107) abundantly filled / plentifully supplied

repress (67) keep down

reprimand (99) severe scolding

reproached (21) criticized

requite (38) return

reserve (86) self-restraint / shyness

residual (71, 117) remaining

resignation (100) give in without resistance

resigned (48, 93, 96, 107) gave in without resistance

resilient (32) capable of bouncing back

resolute (4) firmly determined

resolutions (33) solutions to a problem

resolve (35, 64, 78) firm determination

resolve (81) clear up

resorted (48) turned (for assistance)

respite (82) interval / rest

resplendence (32, 115) brilliant / sparkling

resurrected (35) reintroduced / brought back to life

retain (51, 74, 86, 111) hold on to

retorted (70, 97) replied quickly and sharply

retribution (38, 40, 48) punishment (as revenge) for a wrongdoing

retrogression (77) going backward and (usually) to a worse condition

retrospective (111) looking back

revelation (80) discovery

reveled (24) delighted

reverberations (46) echoing aftereffects

reverence (50) awe and respect

reversion (77) return to an earlier (less developed state)

rickety (1) shaky

rift (80) split or separation / break in friendly relations

righteousness (33, 101) moral standards of good behavior

rite of passage (44) ritual associated with a change of status

ritual (82) ceremony / customarily repeated series of actions

rival (21, 30, 114) competing

robotic (97, 124) mechanical

Romeo (56) (generally) sweetheart

roseate (65) optimistic

rote (104) use of memory (without any deeper thinking-skills applied)

rowdiness (14) disorderly conduct

rubble (124) debris

rudimentary (70) crude / undeveloped

ruminate (6, 103) meditate at length / ponder

safeguards (100) protects

sanatorium (29) institution for the treatment of chronic illness

sanctimonious (72) self-righteous

sanctity (60) sacredness

sanctuary (60) place of refuge

sanguine (65) cheerful

sans (100) without

sardonic (11) cruel and sardonic

sated (40) fully satisfied

savoir faire (18, 61) saying or doing the appropriate things

savoring (9, 100) enjoying / appreciating

savvy (44) shrewd

savvy (67) understand

scholastic (30, 54, 56) relating to school

scrawny (15) skinny

scrutiny (12) close inspection

secured (3, 33) firmly fastened or closed

sedulously (30) diligently

segregated (82) separated

self-aggrandizing (101) exaltation of oneself

self-deprecation (8) belittling of oneself

self-esteem (103) self-respect

selflessly (104) unselfishly

self-righteous (125) complacently / self-satisfied

semi-impervious (14) quite unable to be influenced or changed

seraphic (30) angelic

serendipitous (32) fortunate

servile (69, 121) submissive

sheepishly (9) in an embarrassed manner

shiftless (6) lazy

simulate (38) imitate

simultaneously (115) at the same time

singed (115) burned superficially

singular (19, 48, 100) unique

sinister (69) threatening trouble or harm / evil

slaked (33) quenched

slew (32) large number

slothful (6) sluggish / inactive

sneer (11) look of contempt

snippets (48) small scraps

sniveling (25) crying or sobbing

sober (56) rational

sobering (89) causing one to become sober / bringing one to a serious understanding

socialites (80) socially prominent people

solemn (27, 63, 80) serious and downcast

solicit (4, 76) ask for

solicitous (25) concerned

solidarity (11, 12) unity

solitary (111) single / secluded

sophisticated (30) intricate

sophomoric (54) childish / immature

spawned (54) produced

spewed (forth) (54) threw out

spiffy (12) [slang] fine looking

splendor (32) brilliance / magnificence

spoils (46) plunder

sportively (87) playfully

sprites (46) mischievous spirits

spry (46) lively

SS head honcho (14) (German) state secret police chief

staidly (60) seriously / soberly

star-crossed (81) ill-fated / doomed

stark (56) harsh and blunt

status (61) position

staunch (40) unwavering

stead (103) place

stealthy (67) sneaky

steeped (69) saturated

stemmed (40) derived

stentorian (9) very loud

stereotyped (99, 104) generalize

sterile (121) sanitary

sternly (96) firmly and unyieldingly

stifle (72) hold back / restrain

stimulated (80) aroused

stint (113) allotted duty / period of work

stock (69) common / ordinary

stodgy (72) dull / boring

stoic (96) not showing emotion

straits (99) distress

stratagem (38) strategic move

stunned (91) in shock

suave (1) polite and agreeable

subdued (12, 29, 56, 63) toned down / refraining from showiness

sublimely (50) gloriously superb

subliminally (78) subconsciously

submissively (104) obediently

sub-rosa (16) secret

substantiate (71, 80) verify

substantive (43) significant

subterfuge (14) trickery

subtle (10, 56, 73, 80, 125) not obvious or direct / faint but noticeable

subversive (53) undermining and malicious

subvert (66) undermine

succor (8) assistance in time of need

succumb (90, 99) surrender to a superior force

sufficient (38, 48, 76, 86) adequate

sullenly (96) in a gloomy and resentful manner

summarily (33) immediately

summoned (14, 84) called forth

sumptuous (110) superb

superficial (25, 101) not serious or deep

supplant (71) take the place of

supremacy (53) supreme authority

surmised (87) figured or determined without deeper thought

surreptitious (44, 67) secret / sneaky

surveillance (43) close observation

surveilling (17) watching

sustained (33) maintained **sustenance** (65) support / nourishment

swaggering (45) strutting with an insolent air

sylphic (32) magically graceful

synchronously (100) simultaneously

synergistic (30) collectively powerful

tacitly (11) expressed without words

tact (6) sensitivity in what one says or does

tactfulness (50) use of fact

tactics (48) courses of action

tactlessly (32) lacking tact

tailoring (17) adapting

tangible (48) real / touchable

tantamount (82) equivalent in meaning

taunt (60) challenge through insults

tawny (49) tan / bronze

tedious (67) boring / difficult

teetering (71) seesawing

temerity (44) reckless boldness

temperaments (19) mental / physical character

tempered (81) calmed or moderated / controlled or softened

tempestuous (67) stormy

temporizing (60) stalling

tenets (60) fundamental beliefs

tenuous (58) flimsy and on a weak support ("hanging on by a thread")

tenure (44) term

tepidly (61) unenthusiastically

terminate (33) end

terse (48, 103) effectively concise

testimonial (12) formal statement

thrived (61) flourished

throng (115) crowd

thunderstruck (89) stunned

timely (67) well-timed

tirade (103)

tittered (60) giggled nervously

toiling (9) working hard

torment (122) anguish

toxic (15, 115) poisonous

tranquillity (49) peace

transgressions (33) sins / misdeeds

transpired (1) came to happen / occurred

transubstantiated (103) changed into another form or substance

traumatically (36) causing deep shock

trek (54) difficult travel or journey

tremor (45) shudder

tremulous (35) trembling

trend (15) prevailing style

trepidation (11, 53) nervousness / fear

trifle (67) little bit

trite (104) overused and unimaginative / meaningless and uninteresting

truckle (2) submit

trying (23) difficult

trysts (67) secret meetings

tumultuous (111) chaotic

turbulent (91) stormy

turmoil (19) disturbing confusion

twinge (110) pang / emotional pang

unaffected (45) genuine

unalterable (67, 99, 101) unchangeable or permanent

unappeasable (99) unaccommodating

unbecoming (32, 73, 101) inappropriate

unbridled (96) wild and uncontrolled

unceremoniously (49) rudely abrupt

undaunted (1) not easily discouraged

undefiled (32) unspoiled / pure

underhanded (3, 76) sneaky

undermined (28) weakened and destroyed by wearing away of the foundation

undertaking (38) setting about to do

unearth (80) expose

uneasy (35) uncomfortable

unencumbered (24) unburdened

uneventful (17, 46) ordinary

unexpurgated (78) uncensored

unfeigned (113) sincere

unfettered (107) free

unflagging (18) tireless

unfounded (50) groundless

uninhibitedly (124) not in a restrained manner

unmitigated (113) absolute

unorthodox (101) not traditionally acceptable

unpolluted (33) pure

unrelenting (103) persisting

unrequited (35, 91) not returned

unresolved (90) without a decision

unscathed (43) unharmed

unsubstantiated (50) unverified

untarnished (51, 125) unblemished / untarnished

unveiled (53, 76) disclose

unwarranted (45) unjustified / groundless

unwavering (18, 45) firm and unchanging

unwitting (2, 14, 80) not knowing or aware

upbeat (114) optimistic

uplifted (33) elevated

utter (54, 91) speak

utterly (1) completely

vacuous (49, 104) empty / empty-headed

vagabonds (46) wanderers

valedictorian (86) student who delivers the graduating farewell speech

valiantly (2) courageously

valid (60, 71) logical

validating (82) proving to be accurate and true

vandalous (21) maliciously destructive

vapid (73) dull and stale

variegated (46) multicolored

vendetta (46) bitter feud

veneer (53) outward appearance

venerated (125) respected deeply

vengeance (48) revenge

vengefulness (15) desire for revenge

vent (9, 35, 91) express

venturesome (77) daring and bold

venturousness (46) daring

veracity (6, 113) truthfulness

verge (56) edge / border

vernal (46) youthful

verve (73) artistic spirit

vested (31, 49) clothed

vestiges (124) traces

veteran (11) experienced

vex (46) irritate and worry

vexation (54) irritation

viable (93) workable

vibrancy (100) vigor / energy

vicarious (103) indirect

vicissitudes (29) sudden changes

victor (99) winner

vied (17) competed

vindictive (16, 40) revengeful

virtually (33) practically / essentially

virtuous (33) honorable

virulence (40) spite / malice

vis-à-vis (69) face-to-face

visionary (33) idealistic

vistas (18) scenic view

vitality (32) energy

vituperation (65) scolding

vividly (12, 24) clearly and memorably

vivified (81) added liveliness to

vociferated (15) shouted

vociferous (61) loud

void (17) emptiness

volition (49) free will

volley (78) outburst / barrage

vulnerability (3) openness to injury, criticism or attack

wafted (78) floated

waggish (18) mischievous

waned (29, 86) declined

wanting (19) lacking

Glossary
Fear None But The Innocent

warrant (76) justify

wary (25) cautiously watchful

watchword (48) key word

waxed (34) grew

wayward (33) stubborn and disobedient

weatherworn (73) outdated

welled (45) filled

whelp (15) worthless animal

whence (121) from where

whetted (11) stimulated

whimsically (81) amusingly

whisking (33) rushing

whitewash (125) cover up

wielded (46, 51) carried / exercise

wistfully (121) sadly whimsical

withered (122) dried up so as to lose freshness
  and life

wrath (9) resentful anger

wrathful (35) angry

wreak (46) inflict

wrenching (36) twisting

yearned (34) desired strongly / craved

yield (67) produce / generate

yield (61, 90) surrender / submit

zeal (38) enthusiasm

zealous (1) fanatic

zest (46) gusto

THREE STEPS TO INCREASE VOCABULARY
USING THE HI-LITE SERIES CFR® METHOD

1. **CONFRONT WORDS** in this book that you don't know.

   (Highlight them for added emphasis)

2. **FAMILIARIZE** yourself with their definition.

   (Use the helpful *Glossary*)

3. **REINFORCE** the definitions of newly-acquired words through additional READING.

   (There are two other books in this vocabulary-building trilogy!)

CONFRONT

FAMILIARIZE

REINFORCE
(BY READING)

VERBAL PROFICIENCY IS THE KEY TO BETTER WRITING AND CLEARER COMMUNICATION